T0285121

ALSO BY SHEILA WILLIAMS

Things Past Telling

The Secret Women

Dancing on the Edge of the Roof

The Shade of My Own Tree

On the Right Side of a Dream

Girls Most Likely

No
Better
Time

No
Better
Time

A NOVEL OF THE SPIRITED WOMEN
OF THE SIX TRIPLE EIGHT
CENTRAL POSTAL DIRECTORY BATTALION

Sheila Williams

AMISTAD

An Imprint of HarperCollins*Publishers*

NO BETTER TIME. Copyright © 2024 by Sheila Williams. All rights reserved. Printed in the United States of America. No part of this book may be used or reproduced in any manner whatsoever without written permission except in the case of brief quotations embodied in critical articles and reviews. For information, address HarperCollins Publishers, 195 Broadway, New York, NY 10007.

HarperCollins books may be purchased for educational, business, or sales promotional use. For information, please email the Special Markets Department at SPsales@harpercollins.com.

FIRST EDITION

Library of Congress Cataloging-in-Publication Data has been applied for.

ISBN 978-0-06-330793-3

24 25 26 27 28 LBC 6 5 4 3 2

In honor and memory of the women who served with the 6888th
Central Postal Directory Battalion in World War II.
They had a job to do and they did it.

For Bruce.

May there come across the waters
a path of yellow moonlight
to bring you safely home.

JOHN O'DONOHUE, "BEANNACHT"

No
Better
Time

A FINE MESS

February 1945
On deck
Aboard the RMS *Queen Mary*
Somewhere in the North Atlantic

T hom, you look green."

Leila Branch was standing only a few feet away but her voice sounded like an echo, hollow and distorted as if it was coming out of a cave.

Dorothy Thom's grip tightened on the railing and she closed her eyes, going against the oft-quoted advice *not* to close one's eyes. The ship rose, then fell. Her stomach rose and fell. She inhaled, then exhaled. Both were painful.

"I'm too dark to be green," she said to her friend in a raspy voice. Opening her eyes, she glanced at Leila, then smiled—or intended to smile. Her stomach didn't want her to cooperate. "Now, *you* look green . . . split-pea-soup green."

Leila swallowed hard.

"Thank you for that." She coughed. *Oh, no . . .*

"I'm with you," Dorothy murmured. She exhaled again. Not helpful.

The two women locked eyes for a moment. Remembering the pointers given to them by their sergeant before boarding the dull-gray ("the better the U-boats won't see us") ship with trepidation, they turned their gazes toward the horizon. A horizon that Sergeant Layne had assured them would be flat and unmoving. It wasn't. As a matter of fact, the instructive Sergeant Layne was at this very moment below deck in her bunk moaning from seasickness.

"So much for her advice," growled Leila. She inhaled deeply again. *Okay, that wasn't bad.* Blinking, she scanned the horizon. "Remind me . . ."

"Remind me . . ." Dorothy parroted. "Remind you of what?"

"Why did we sign up for this?"

Despite the desperate feeling in her stomach, Dorothy managed a chuckle.

"There's no 'we' here, Branch," she said, using Leila's surname in the way that the sergeant did. "We aren't Laurel and Hardy. It's not my fault that . . ."

"We're in another fine mess?" Leila interjected. She nodded toward the sea. "It was your suggestion."

Dorothy chuckled again, then tapped her mate on the shoulder.

"There will be a mess if you don't lean over that railing more."

Leila took Dorothy's advice, then closed her eyes and turned her pale, crab apple–green face toward a sliver of sunlight that had just emerged from behind sullen, light-gray clouds.

"I know why *you* signed up," she said, finally. "You said that you wanted an adventure."

Dorothy coughed, then swallowed.

"Uh. Oh. Did I say that?"

Now it was Leila's turn to smile, although Dorothy thought her expression was more like a grimace.

"You did, Private, Miss Spelman 1938. You wanted to go abroad. So here you are, almost abroad. There are two ways to get there, and your rank isn't high enough for one of them. So . . ." Leila gestured toward the formidable-looking Atlantic.

"So," Dorothy said with misery in her voice. "While you . . ."

Leila shook her head slowly, remembering the bitter exchange of words she'd had with her mother after she told her that she'd enlisted. "While I"—she stopped and cleared her throat—"I didn't want an adventure. I just wanted the chance to be something more than Pearl Branch's girl down the street who got herself knocked up . . ."

"In the family way," Dorothy interrupted.

Leila gave herself permission to grin, hoping that she wouldn't regret it.

"That too. Without a husband anywhere in sight, hardly enough schooling to count for much, and only a maid's job to keep her. Oh, and no prospects of doing better or getting more for herself and her boy."

Now it was Dorothy's turn to grin and hoot with laughter.

"Well, aren't we a pair?" She pulled a handkerchief from her pocket and blew her nose. "I'm feeling a little better. What about you?"

Leila shrugged. Strangely enough, she, too, was feeling more human.

"Yes, I am. Should be able to fall in and pass review without throwing up on Sergeant's shoes."

"Ha! Assuming she's feeling well enough to show up herself!"

The women laughed and began to straighten their coats and smooth the fabric of their rough khaki work uniforms.

"Uh-huh. Anyway, the ocean seems a bit calmer," Dorothy remarked.

But when the gods wish to punish you, they shatter your assumptions. A swell paid a visit and nudged the hull of the former-luxury-liner-turned-troop-transport-vessel RMS *Queen Mary* as it parted the waters.

Leila ran toward the railing.

"No, it's not!"

Dorothy sighed and handed her friend a handkerchief. Leila studied it briefly before extending her hand.

"It's clean," Dorothy said through clenched teeth. "I always keep two in my pockets."

"Whose fault is this again?" Leila groaned, her voice sounding pitiful.

Dorothy rolled her eyes. *Bad idea.* All of a sudden, she was feeling miserable again.

"Roosevelt," she said. It was the first name that came to mind. Leila nodded.

"That's right. Let's blame Roosevelt."

OUT OF THE COCOON

December 8, 1941
12:25 p.m. Eastern Daylight Time
Spelman College Library
Atlanta, Georgia

Dorothy Thom was an experienced teacher. She adored children, and they adored her. She was revered like a fairy godmother by the third graders she taught at Margaret M. Washington Primary School in Miami, Florida. She led the mischievous little ones from skinned knees to arithmetic and reading without them realizing that they were learning something important. Her colleagues enjoyed her company; her principal considered her a gem and wished that all of his teachers were as accomplished. Her salary—though not as high as those paid to white teachers in town—was at least enough to keep her in smart clothes and high heels, a necessity for Dorothy, who stood five feet and one-half inches in bare feet. She would add an extra half inch; it boosted her confidence.

And yet she had never been happier than when she left her teaching job in Florida to become the librarian in the freshman reading room of Atlanta's Spelman College. Her father, Dr. Thom, a professor of theology, was disappointed. He preferred that Dorothy stay in Florida so that he could keep an eye on her. But her mother, Eva, now living in Cleveland, thought it was a good move—Atlanta was a vibrant town, and vibrancy was something that Eva appreciated. Atlanta was cosmopolitan. And the Spelman Library, unlike the underpopulated library at the local normal school in St. Augustine, Florida, maintained a collection of works in French, books that fed Dorothy's obsession. She borrowed her favorites, anything by Flaubert or Dumas, so often and kept them for so long that the librarian issued a warning citation.

She'd taken her degree from Spelman with a double major in English literature and French. Now, on her break, she sat in a quiet reading nook, elbow bent, chin in palm, her mind a thousand miles away, contemplating the moral dilemma of Madame Emma Bovary. *En français*, of course.

But it wasn't only Emma's mental landscape that Dorothy contemplated. Flaubert had transported her to the French countryside, verdant and fresh after spring rains, fragrant with the perfume of lilac. The late afternoon sun warmed deep-blue and aubergine grapes while, in the distance, orioles were in flight, performing pirouettes in a final ballet before taking their exit southward to Italy . . .

"Miss Thom! Miss Thom!"

The calling of her name and quickstep click of heels on the hardwood floor cut through the sublime aura of the moment like the grinding of a locomotive's wheels against a track.

"Yes? What is it?"

The student was gasping for breath as if she'd just finished a relay race.

"Miss Patterson says come. Come now! To the break room. The president is about to speak. On the radio!"

No need to say which president; there had only been the one for the past eight years. And no need to say what the news would be. The nation had anticipated an announcement for weeks. Everyone knew that the United States was edging toward a war with Germany.

Dorothy closed the book carefully, slipping a piece of paper inside to save her place, and quickly left her seat, following the girl who was running down the aisle toward the back of the library. As Dorothy approached, she heard static emanating from the large brown box as Dr. Read, the college president, adjusted the dials in an attempt to get a clearer signal. There was tension and excitement in the room. Both had been building for several years on the Spelman campus, in Atlanta, and across the United States and the world. The stories were everywhere on the radio and in the papers: the bombing of Britain, haunting images of London, and the odd, static-tinged voice of Churchill, which was now familiar to American ears. Murmurs about the Japanese in the east. Disturbing reports about military campaigns and atrocities in Germany and in Poland, where an animated, mustached man raised his arm and spoke of glory and a superior race. No need to say which race he considered superior: the Negro press had covered the 1936 Olympics in Berlin. Jesse Owens was a hero to his people at home, but the mustached man had other opinions.

Dorothy's stomach was in knots as she maneuvered herself into the break room and found a seat on the edge of a desk. War meant soldiers. And Dorothy had two brothers, several cousins, and many friends of fighting age. The women whispered loudly among themselves. Dr. Read put one finger to her lips and the room quieted. The radio sputtered, then a familiar voice broke through the static.

"Mr. Vice President, and Mr. Speaker, and Members of the Senate and House of Representatives: Yesterday, December 7, 1941—a date which will live in infamy—the United States of America was suddenly and deliberately attacked by naval and air forces of the Empire of Japan."

From that moment, Dorothy added a new word to her vocabulary, one that she had rarely used before: *casualties*.

* * *

December 8, 1941
12:35 p.m. Eastern Daylight Time
Pearl Branch's Boardinghouse
Dayton, Ohio

"Leila? Leila! Get the baby!"

Pearl Branch poked her head out of the parlor door, her attention split between the earthshaking news coming across the radio and the sound of a screaming baby. One ear was trained on President Roosevelt's voice, her other on the squalling. Pearl frowned and yelled again, "Leila! The baby's cryin'! Loud enough to wake the dead. Where *are* you?"

"Comin', Momma!"

"Goodness gracious, hurry up. I can't hear the president."

Leila had been sleeping. Napping, really. There'd been no such thing as sleep since Paris was born. Naps were all she got, and they were always too short. When Paris slept, Leila napped. Or at least she closed her eyes. Rest was for the weary. Was that from the Bible? If so, why didn't Leila get any rest? She was surely weary. The baby hiccuped, inhaled, then screamed again. Leila felt the front of her blouse. *Darn.*

"Leila! The baby's hungry! Stick your titty in his mouth and shut him up! Before he wakes Mr. Shaw! He's working third this week! 'Sides, I can't hear the radio! The president's . . ."

Oh, well, if it's the president.

Leila rolled her eyes, glad that she was in her room and that her mother couldn't see her. Being pregnant had been bad enough. Having a baby—and not a husband—was worse. But sticking your boob into the mouth of a screaming infant was horrible. Paris took a moment to catch his breath, then latched onto the nipple. Leila cringed. Breastfeeding was disgusting.

There was a knock at the door that coincided with Pearl's entrance into the room.

"Well, it 'bout time! Gracious!" She walked over to the bed and stroked her grandson's head. "He's a sweetie pie, but Lord, that boy is loud. I just hope I don't lose any boarders."

Leila adjusted her son to settle him more comfortably into the crook of her arm.

"What's he talking about?"

"Shhh!"

Pearl's lip settled into a line as she clicked on the radio setting on the night table next to Leila's bed.

President Roosevelt's voice filled the room.

"No matter how long it may take us to overcome this premeditated invasion, the American people in their righteous might will win through to absolute victory. I believe that I interpret the will of the Congress and of the people when I assert that we will not only defend ourselves to the uttermost but will make it very certain that this form of treachery shall never again endanger us. Hostilities exist. There is no blinking at the fact that our people, our territory, and our interests are in grave danger . . ."

Leila Branch sat straight in the chair, her eyes and attention riveted to the small ivory-colored box, oblivious to her nursing son. "Defend ourselves . . . Hostilities . . ." Born after the First World War, Leila had rarely heard these words either in conversation or over the airwaves. What did they mean? How did one defend oneself against "hostilities"? When she'd bothered to listen, which wasn't often, the teenage Leila had heard the old folks droning on about the "WWI" and what may or may not have taken place (and by whom) as the Rough Riders ascended a mound called San Juan Hill during the Spanish-American conflict. The voices of her uncles merged with those of any male lodger in the good graces of her mother (and current on rent payments) to debate the merits of this strategy or the folly of that one. What colored soldiers did and didn't get credit for and the danger involved. The history went in one of Leila's ears and out the other. What did any of it have to do with her? She'd smiled, said good morning or good evening to whichever gentleman spoke, then disappeared quickly into her mother's kitchen to escape.

But now? With a small son nestled against her chest, Leila was at attention. War. She had a son. Yes, he was only a baby, but these things could drag on. Hostilities. She knew enough about the German man, ferocious in his speaking, and the ominous rumors emerging from the other side of the world to know that this was serious. She felt an unfamiliar emotion: fear. It was all too real now, what people meant when they said "life or death." Sons went to war. Men died or were maimed. Or, like her uncle Berkeley, were gassed and never the same again. This war, whatever it was really about and wherever it took place, was too close. With Paris's birth, it had become personal. Leila's breath caught in her throat as she listened.

*   *   *

Five hundred miles away in an alcove that served as the break room of the Spelman College library, perched on the edge of a desk, Dorothy Thom was as still as a marble statue, but her heart was racing. Unblinkingly, she listened to the president's address as it gathered the steam needed to inform the nation that it was at war.

War. War? War!

Dorothy's stomach quivered with excitement. Born in 1915, she hadn't been old enough to process the events surrounding the last war, what some called the "Great War." But she'd heard about it from her uncles and older male cousins, from a family friend who'd been gassed in France. From her father who had registered but whose poor vision had not allowed him to serve militarily and who had been a chaplain. She'd heard about the 369th Infantry known as the "Harlem Hellfighters," men pulled from the cities and plains of the United States to serve in the trenches of France, earning the highest praise and awarded military honors, including la Croix de Guerre. And in the back of her mind, she thought of an old lady who went to Aunt Denie's church in Atlanta, oh, what was her name? Mrs. Something, small and fair with bright light-brown eyes, a marvelous storyteller who had served in the Red Cross nursing corps in France. The stories Mrs. What's-Her-Name had told were mesmerizing. Even more mesmerizing because she spoke of the various kinds of work that had to be done to support the fighting men. Women's work. It wasn't all battlefields and guns. The hospital corps. The supply lines. Quartermaster's duties. Transportation. Red tape and paperwork. There were other jobs to be done besides load, aim, and pull a trigger. Dorothy wondered. Could *she* do that work?

"With the unbounding determination of our people—we will gain the inevitable triumph—so help us God. I ask that the Congress declare that since the unprovoked and dastardly attack by

Japan on Sunday, December 7, 1941, a state of war has existed between the United States and the Japanese Empire."

On December 11, the United States, by act of Congress, declared war on Germany. And two young women living hundreds
of miles apart wondered what the world was coming to and what it
would mean for them.

Dorothy Eugenia Is Bored

February 1945
Aboard the RMS *Queen Mary*

t took a moment, several moments, for Dorothy and Leila to make the journey to the starboard side of the ship, making sure that they replaced their helmets and fastened their life jackets before falling in for review by Lieutenant Corbin. Dorothy knew, without checking a mirror, that she looked like death warmed over. Poor Leila, who'd suffered more, looked worse. But "needs must," Dorothy said to herself, adopting a phrase learned in an "English ways and phrases" lecture she'd attended at Ft. Oglethorpe. She took deep breaths and coughed because the sea air was briny and cold. Then she tucked her chin and pushed forward, holding her cap against the wind with one hand. Walking at her side, Leila did the same, her pasty complexion regaining a somewhat normal shade thanks also to the chilly spray from the sea.

Bad as this journey was, it would soon be over, Dorothy mused, and it wasn't useful to dwell on the fact that, at some point in the future, there would be another Atlantic crossing on the return trip. What was useful to dwell on was that they were traveling on the best ship (Leila still called it a "boat") possible for the journey. The British-owned RMS *Queen Mary* was larger than the ill-fated *Titanic* and fast. She cut through the Atlantic waves at up to twenty-nine knots. With twelve decks and built to be the most luxurious of the oceangoing liners, she wasn't very luxurious now, stripped of her gold-trimmed accoutrements, expensive carpets, and priceless art. Inside, all of the glamour had been pulled out, crated, and taken away. The well-appointed staterooms swapped their feather mattresses for bunk beds three levels high. Without her "cosmetics" and with her portholes blacked out, she was painted a light-gray camo to mask the Cunard red, white, and black, and to blend easily into the fog and cold mists of the North Atlantic. The "Gray Ghost," as she was fondly called, had been transformed like Cinderella in reverse from a luxury liner to a transport loaned to the Americans to ferry troops back and forth across the Atlantic. She zigzagged along her course to throw off the German submarines. Her elegance, size, and speed irked the small German man, who placed a bounty on her bow—the equivalent of $250,000 in American currency and the Iron Cross to any U-boat captain who sank her. That was in 1942. It was now February 1945. So far, so good.

The Ghost was massive and intimidating now that her sunbathing decks had been retrofitted with equipment and munitions. It took some time for the seasick privates to reach the deck where their company had gathered. They rounded a corridor once used as a smoking porch in prewar times now transformed, its elegant windows removed to support the imposing barrels of antiaircraft guns.

"We need bread crumbs," Dorothy quipped.

Eventually, figures of their sister WACs emerged from the gloom, the women moving quickly to get into formation. Leila tapped Dorothy on the shoulder as she stepped into her place. Dorothy winked at her, then turned her attention to the front and the officer in charge.

"Attention!" It was said that Connie Corbin's contralto could wake the mummies in Egypt. Known to her family and friends in Ashland, Kentucky, as "Little Connie Jean," the lieutenant was a powerhouse of energy with the voice of a cannon in a tiny package only five feet, two inches tall.

"Fall in!"

Dorothy pulled herself straight and stamped her feet against the cold. She couldn't feel her toes. Smiling slightly, she settled into attention stance with "eyes front, chin up, shoulders back."

No. If there was anyone to blame for her current predicament—if "blame" was the right word—it wasn't Leila or anyone, really, but Dorothy herself.

She had gotten herself into this fine mess. And all because she was bored. It had been that way since she was a child. Where Dorothy was concerned, boredom could be dangerous. Somehow, she always ended up in a situation, usually after being told that she could not do something that she was only doing because she was bored. Because the whatever-it-was that Dorothy wanted to do was, of course, interesting, exciting, and probably a tad dangerous but definitely guaranteed not to be boring.

"Dorothy, you can't do that! It isn't ladylike!" This from her eldest sister, who was the authority of all things "ladylike."

"Girls can't do that," said with glee in the singsong voice of one of her brothers, who was happy that his adventurous sister was prohibited by gender from doing "it," whatever "it" was, because Dorothy was better at "it" than he was.

"No respectable colored woman should be doing that." This edict from her grandfather, Jack, called "Big Dad" by the family, not because of his height but his towering will. In Big Dad's opinion—and his opinions were always respected, even when not acted upon—respectability was everything.

And then there were the inevitable litanies of warnings that Dorothy was either too-this or too-that added to "Whatever gave you that idea?" then topped liked icing on a cake with the question that Dorothy hated most: "Who do you think you are?" In her view, the landscape of her childhood was thickly populated with incidents designed to limit the boundaries of her life. And Dorothy wanted nothing to do with limits or boundaries.

The time Dorothy used a chair for a stepladder to reach the white crockery milk jug on the top shelf of Mother's pantry, she'd heard something rattling when Father placed it out of reach and, of course, she was intrigued. Dorothy just had to know what was in it. And since Rosa—the only one of her sisters tall enough to reach the jug—wouldn't help, Dorothy decided to go after it herself. And she almost got away with it.

But the chair was old and its woven cane seat was worn and unraveling. So when Dorothy's foot slipped between the stretched-out strands of cane, she lost her balance and fell. Her sisters, who'd watched from the safety of the kitchen door, shrieked with laughter, then issued edicts of blame.

"Aw . . . look what you done," Hattie's voice overflowed with delight.

"What you *have* done," Rosa corrected her. But she was just as delighted.

"What's going on in there?" Their mother did not sound delighted.

"Nothing!" the chorus replied.

"What broke?"

"Dorothy did it!" the Hattie-Rosa duet chimed with glee.

"I just wanted to see what was in it" was Dorothy's defense.

It was the same answer she gave when she fell out of the old, gnarled oak tree in her grandfather's yard in Eatonton. From this adventure, she'd sprained her shoulder, skinned both knees, and scraped the skin from her palms. Dorothy knew that climbing the tree was dangerous, but the hollow in the tree was inviting and she wanted to see if there was treasure in it. There wasn't, only yellow jackets. It was a miracle that she wasn't stung.

"That gal's nose gonna get her in a heap of troubles someday," Big Dad observed to a neighbor a few days after Dorothy's abrupt descent from the oak tree. "Been telling her that. Her momma too."

Doc Jones snorted, then spat out a vicious-looking plug of tobacco that nearly landed on the toe of his friend's left boot. Jack scowled at him.

"Can't tell 'em nothin', Jack, you know that. She'll figger it out herself. Don't woke 'em, let 'em slept."

When Dorothy was nine, her parents separated, and she and her sisters went to stay with their aunt and uncle in Atlanta, while their brothers remained with their father in Florida. The visit with Aunt Denie morphed into an extended stay, which solidified into a ten-year residency. Atlanta, larger than Dublin, Georgia, where the girls spent their early years, had much more to offer in the way of fine schools, shopping, and culture. But even so, Dorothy was restless.

One Sunday when she was ten, she stood with her sisters in her aunt's front hall as they prepared to leave for church. As she pulled her gloves on, Denie gave the girls a cursory glance then exclaimed, "What in Hades!" and nearly had an apoplectic fit. The dainty ruffled skirt of Dorothy's just-out-of-the-box pale peach-colored dress was marked by bold red stains, as were her white lace-trimmed anklet socks.

Denie bent down to touch a stain that was vivid red orange in color and streaked with small seeds. Her jaw set, her eyes—near black in color and ominous—bored into those of her niece. "How many of them did you eat?" she demanded, referring to her tomatoes.

"Just one, Aunt Denie. I'm sorry! They looked so good. I wanted to see if they taste as good as they look." She hoped that flattery worked. "And I didn't have anything else to do. I was already dressed and waiting for Hat to finish . . ." Dorothy let her voice trail off as she sent a baleful look in Hattie's direction. "She always takes forever. And I got *bored.* So I grabbed the saltshaker and ate one." She looked down at the soiled front of her dress. "I don't think I spoiled it. Maybe if I just . . ."

But the hand she'd intended to rub across the front of the now-ruined dress was batted away by her aunt.

"Don't. Do. That."

Not that Denie was under any illusion that her tomatoes weren't excellent in appearance and flavor, but their juice did not belong on the front skirt of the dress she'd bought for Dorothy from Rich's in downtown Atlanta. It had cost the earth!

When Dorothy was bored, things just, well, happened. But as she got older, she learned to make things happen—to her benefit. The *Queen Mary* swayed as if to agree and add, "Next time, be careful what you wish for." Dorothy swallowed. She felt this movement from the top of her head to the soles of her frozen feet.

Leila Branch stamped her feet too. Her toes were frozen even though she was wearing arctics, the thick, unwieldy army-issue boots that were supposed to be impervious to damp and cold. *So much for that.* She curled, then uncurled her fingers that were stiff despite the thick woolen gloves and wriggled her nose. She hoped to God that she didn't sneeze. But on second thought, that might not be a bad thing. It was frigid here in the North Atlantic and Leila wasn't sure that her nose was still on her face, because she couldn't feel it. Come to that, she couldn't feel anything. Even her stomach was frozen, but maybe *that* was a good thing.

Leila tried to focus on Lieutenant Corbin's commands. Maybe they would warm her up. Yes, this was a fine mess, although whether it was actually *fine* could be debated. But it was a mess, no doubt about that. And, like Dorothy, Leila had no one to blame but herself. No one had forced her to hitch a ride to the recruiting office in downtown Dayton. No one had held a gun to her head and ordered her to sign her name at the *X*. So, in that regard, she and Dorothy were alike.

But unlike Doro, Leila hadn't enlisted because she was bored. She hadn't been inspired by the luminous words of a recruiter or encouraged by what she'd read about Mrs. Bethune in the *Call & Post*. Leila didn't long to hear Big Ben or walk in the footsteps of Flaubert, whoever he was. Sure, she'd often thought about what it would be like to actually be in the city she'd named her son after. But no, Leila hadn't joined the Women's Army Auxiliary Corps to do her part, travel abroad, or have an adventure.

She joined because she had a child to support, no education to speak of, no skills of any kind, and a burning desire to get out of her mother's boardinghouse and out of Dayton.

ONE QUESTION

Winter 1942
Spelman College
Atlanta, Georgia

Dorothy's great adventure had an unadventurous beginning. She graduated from high school and went to Spelman College to "improve" herself by taking a double major in English literature and French. In the spring of 1938, she prepared herself for graduation and for what might come next.

"Time she got herself a husband," Big Dad had grumbled to Denie when she and Dorothy drove out from Atlanta to the country to visit the old man. "What does a colored woman need with a degree in French?"

A husband? Just remembering her grandfather's comment made Dorothy's stomach ache. It sent her aunt Denie into a giggling fit.

It was a warm, pleasant day in Atlanta, the azaleas bloomed red, violet, and white, and Denie's so-called English garden was showing the artistry of its designer as carefully placed plants and blossoms emerged from winter slumber, their appearances choreographed. The front porch had been swept and mopped, the covers removed from the wicker furniture. Denie Hawke's front porch was more luxuriously appointed than most folks' parlors. Like an exotic queen from ages past, she held court in a cushioned rocking chair, cooling her face with a Japanese fan while sipping a cocktail of her own creation: ice-cold lemonade with a splash of a clear liquor imported from Russia, accessorized with a sprig of mint.

"I don't know what's so funny," Dorothy growled. "This is my future we're talking about."

"Listen, child," Denie said, taking a sip of her drink, coughing, then taking another sip. "You don't have a thing to worry about. The world is in the palm of your hand, you just don't know it. When your mother and I came out of school? We had one choice." She reached out and grabbed her niece's hand, then turned it over. "Speaking of . . . Dorothy! What did I tell you about your fingernails? Manicure. Today. Before you do anything else, y'hear? Looks like you've been digging potatoes!" Denie's expression of disapproval spoke volumes. "There's a bottle of Cutex Riot Red on my dressing table. Brand-new. Use it!"

"Yes, ma'am," Dorothy murmured.

"Now, what was I sayin'? Oh, yes. Choices. At least you have some. Listen to me, not to Big Dad, bless his heart and I love him to death. Papa means well but he's from another time. If you decide to get married, you make the decision. Choose a husband carefully. Scientifically." She picked up the frosted cocktail glass slowly, her perfectly painted coral-red nails gleaming in the sunlight. Denie's dark eyes bored into Dorothy's. "So I am not talking about that Cunningham boy, understand?"

Dorothy was almost too stunned to say anything. How did Denie know that she was seeing . . . stupid question. Her aunt had spies everywhere.

"What's wrong with Henry Cunningham?" she fired back.

Her aunt snorted.

"In the first place, his table manners are atrocious." Denie's face hardened into a marble mask of disapproval. "He chews with his mouth open and doesn't know what to do with a napkin."

Dorothy laughed.

"That's not a capital offense."

"It should be," Denie commented. "And his head is shaped like a pineapple."

Dorothy howled with laughter.

"If it wasn't for that little talk we had a few years ago . . ."

"Denie!"

"As I was saying? If not for that 'talk,' you might have one or two pineapple-headed babies by now."

Dorothy tried to give her aunt the evil eye and failed, her moment of pique dissolving into giggles. She couldn't help herself. Her imagination had conjured the image of a small child bearing a benign but pleasant expression imprinted onto a pineapple-shaped head.

"But the way Big Dad carries on . . ."

Denie skimmed the rim of her glass with one long painted fingernail. "It isn't that. Your grandfather is many things . . ."

"A tyrant. Stingy. Stone-headed," Dorothy interrupted.

"True, all true," Denie said, nodding. "But remember who he is and when he's from. Hardly five years old when Sherman came through the farm, just a little boy, holding Grandma Mahala's hand. He watched as she was beaten. He saw other colored women taken advantage of. And he swore to keep that from happening to his wife and daughters. Or granddaughters. Safety and security mean a lot to him." Denie paused. "In his mind, that means marriage to an educated, cultured, churchgoing man . . ."

"Preferably Baptist," Dorothy said, grinning.

Her aunt grinned back.

"Definitely Baptist. But it's up to you, Dorothy. Decide what you want. Stand up for yourself and step out. See what the world offers. The only other choice is to let someone else run your life and push you down a narrow road." Denie's dark gaze never left Dorothy's face. "Your. Choice."

Dorothy remembered this conversation some months later as she sat on a hard wooden chair in the office of Dr. Florence Read, president of Spelman College. Across the desk from her, sitting in Dr. Read's usual place, was a young woman wearing a serious expression and dressed in a dark olive khaki skirt suit accessorized with insignias, stripes, chevrons, and badges. Her hat rested on the desk in front of her. Her hands, their slender fingers unadorned by rings, were elegant yet strong-looking and her short nails were unpainted. Her face was round but not plump, and dark feather-like brows framed her light brown eyes. Her dark brown hair was elegantly styled into a chignon. The woman's smile was friendly and the tenor of her voice put Dorothy at ease, but there was a thread of steel supporting it. This was not a woman to put up with foolishness. Her remarks during chapel were inspiring yet concise. Her intent was clear. There was a place for educated Negro women in the Women's Army Auxiliary Corps. Enthusiastic applause marked the completion of her presentation and the women of Spelman were impressed and formed a queue to meet with the recruiter after chapel. Message received: There was a war on. It was time to do one's part.

Dorothy was so wrapped up in her own thoughts that she hardly noticed that the woman in the army uniform had finished her speech. Yet she'd heard every word and marked each move that the woman had made, noted each crease in the crisp uniform, the enunciation of every word that emerged from the officer's lips—because she was an officer! Not to mention the smart color of her lipstick. *Helena Rubinstein? Elizabeth Arden?* Dorothy thought. Her mind spun off into many directions as she sought to narrow her focus to the next point of action, toward her next adventure. For a moment, Dorothy realized that she was heading into deep water. This was not child's play. This was the US Army, and the country was at war. But had she been looking into a mirror, she would have seen a broad smile across her own face.

This could be fun!

The woman sitting across from Dorothy cleared her throat and made the appearance of adjusting the proximity of the wheeled office chair to the desk. She smiled at Dorothy and narrowed her eyes slightly but not in an unkind way. She moistened her lips but didn't disturb the soft mauve lipstick that she'd applied and that Dorothy so admired. She unfolded her hands and placed them, palms down, on the desk, then after a moment, she folded them again. Finally, she cleared her throat once more.

"Miss Thom?"

Dorothy's attention shifted back to the present moment.

"Yes . . . ma'am." It seemed strange to call the woman "ma'am" when she was not much younger or older than Dorothy. But the uniform she wore demanded formality.

The woman's smile widened.

"I asked you a question."

Dorothy's heart jumped into her throat.

"Oh! I'm sorry. Um . . . what was the question again?"

The woman bit her lip to keep from laughing.

"I asked if *you* had any questions."

Dorothy felt her cheeks warming. "Yes. Yes, I do. One question."

The woman nodded.

"Please."

"Do you think I'll get to go abroad?"

It would be a few years before Dorothy would learn the truth. That on the day she asked the question, Captain Dovey M. Johnson had no idea.

The US Army had not yet figured out what they would do with the women who'd signed up for what would become the Women's Army Auxiliary Corps. Congress and the US Army brass had not wanted to enlist women at all. From their way of thinking, it was foolish. Women? In uniform? Certainly the Brits and the French had done it. But this was Uncle Sam's Army. What purpose could they serve? As cooks? Cleaners? There were enlisted men who did these chores and did them well. Pour tea? Darn socks? Entertain the soldiers? Seriously?

Another one of "that woman's" nutty ideas, some thought, "that woman" being Eleanor Roosevelt. The brass pushed back as hard as they could, where they could. Political pressure was applied. A bill to create a women's corps was introduced to Congress in May 1941 by Representative Edith Nourse of Massachusetts. Without the backing of the war department, it went nowhere for months. After the bombing of Pearl Harbor, the uncomfortable reality was that everyone might be needed on all fronts in multiple capacities, men *and* women. The bill was excavated from the budget office.

The army was unprepared for the response. Young women wanting to "do their part" joined in numbers that exceeded the initial recruitment goals. Their energy and enthusiasm was over-whelming. The army had no idea what to *do*. Training, assign-ments, duties, officer corps, uniforms for women? This was unexplored terrain. Some base commanders protested that the presence of women would dampen morale and erode discipline. And that went double for the thirty-nine women of the Third Platoon, First Company of the WAAC, the first Negro women to be trained as officers, and all the women who followed them. In their civilian lives, they were schoolteachers, beauticians, cooks, textile workers, farm laborers, and law students. They were insurance agents and home ec teachers. They were maids and secretaries. But they were Negroes. The US military was segregated. The answer to Dorothy's question was shrouded in a fog that would not clear for at least two years. But Captain Johnson chose to be optimistic. After all, the patron saint and guardian angel of the Third Platoon was the indefatigable Dr. Mary McLeod Bethune, friend of Mrs. Roosevelt. Anything was possible.

Dovey Johnson smiled.

"Yes, of course."

Dorothy beamed.

"Where do I sign up, er, ma'am? Miss Johnson?"

Dovey Johnson stood and extended her hand.

"Captain. It's captain."

OF INFINITE VARIETY

Fall 1942
Dayton, Ohio

Cooks, teachers, secretaries, and sharecroppers' daughters signed their allegiance to the Women's Army Auxiliary Corps, as did the Alpha Kappa Alpha sorors, whose parents were born into DuBois's talented tenth. The women, a kaleidoscope of colors, abilities, resumes, and dreams, came from all points of the American landscape from the Louisiana bayou to the Appalachian foothills, from San Francisco Bay to the flatlands of central Ohio. They were married, unmarried, divorced, widowed. They were a college librarian and a hotel maid.

Leila knew about the Women's Army Auxiliary Corps, everybody did. "The war" and anything connected to it was all people talked about. Radio broadcasters fell over themselves to report the "breaking news" from the front, whether it was breaking or not. The war was all anyone heard about. It was in all the newspapers, so it was all people read about. And Leila's mother, Pearl Branch, had three papers delivered at minimum every day—the two Dayton dailies plus the *Enquirer* out of Cincinnati and the *Call & Post* on the weekend. Leila was no scholar—in school she hadn't felt the need to pay much attention to her studies, preferring dances and swing music—which accounted in part for her current predicament. But this—this war and everything to do with it—was different. Factories that used to make cash registers and automobile parts now ran twenty-four hours a day, seven days a week, manufacturing parts for tanks, army trucks, bomb sights, and propellers. Some of her school friends and their mothers and aunts now worked on the assembly lines. Her Springfield cousins, known as "the boys," enlisted in the army. Her Detroit cousin joined the navy. Everyone she knew was jazzed up over the war. Leila was intrigued too, but she didn't see how she could fit into the war effort unless she took a job at the Delco plant on the north side of town because they were hiring. That prospect was not enticing.

So it was surprising that, of all places, it was the buzz at church that drew her in.

Pearl put in an appearance at Pine Street AME Church once a month or so, too busy on Sundays running the boardinghouse to attend more often. But she took her churchgoing seriously.

"It's good for business," she said in her own defense when Leila teased her. If ever there was a nonbeliever, Pearl was it. But she was protective of her carefully crafted status in the community as a respectable "widow woman," and her church attendance, even if occasional, was required to support the image. Fortunately for Pearl, Jonny Branch hadn't been seen in Dayton since Leila was a toddler, so no one remembered exactly what he looked like, and the sepia photo of him that Pearl displayed was blurry at best. With Jonny's people being from New Orleans and Jonny being a non-communicator, as in he didn't send letters or postcards, it could be said that Pearl struck gold when she married him, if in fact she ever did. There was no one in town who'd heard from him in over fifteen years, and therefore, no one could voice the inconvenient fact that Jonny wasn't dead but alive and well, working as a boiler-maker on the railroad and living in St. Louis with his wife and five children. No one but Pearl.

"It's good for business," she repeated as she extracted a hat from its enormous box. "And today *you're* going with me."

Leila protested—she disliked the services, disliked the preacher, and especially disliked the gossipy parishioners who looked down on her. Not to mention the misery of bringing two-year-old Paris with her. Pine Street AME had no nursery on the first Sunday, which guaranteed an hour and a half of wrestling with the toddler in her lap.

But her mother was in no mood to argue, so Leila resigned herself to a morning of frustration. But this morning, after the hymn and before what would likely be the most tedious sermon ever given, Reverend Davis made the announcements: no Sunday school next week due to a Labor Day festival, please keep Sister Whatever and Brother Who The Heck Cares in your prayers, General Motors is hiring men and women . . .

Leila blanked out most of the rest; she and Paris were playing a game of throw the toy down so that Mommy can pick it up and you can throw it down again, but a few phrases crept into her consciousness:

Mrs. Bethune . . .

. . . girls do their part . . .

Women's Army Auxiliary Corps . . .

And from the pew behind her, loud whispers:

Mamie enlisted . . . going to Ft. Des Moines, wherever that is . . .

Kansas, you dope . . .

I thought it was in Iowa . . .

. . . my cousin Elma loves it . . .

. . . paid twenty-one dollars a month!

Leila almost dropped her son.

Twenty-one dollars a month!

What could she do with twenty-one dollars in wages every month? Leila retrieved Paris's squeaky toy and inclined her head to the side, the better to hear the chatterboxes sitting behind her. One woman said that the uniforms were itchy and didn't fit. Her cousin had said that the food wasn't great but wasn't bad, whatever that meant. You could sign up at the recruiting office in the post office building downtown . . .

With twenty-one dollars coming in every month, Leila could pay for Paris's keep and help her mother with the bills. She would have enough to put by for later, maybe even get her own place. She would have enough to start a savings for Paris so that he could go to a good school or even college someday. If the chatterboxes were to be believed, Leila could do better for herself and her son by joining the army than she ever would if she worked her whole life as a maid. Any second thoughts she had were quickly put out of her head.

Leila worked overtime at the hotel on Wednesday. Asked her mother's friend, Mrs. Battle, if she would watch Paris for an extra hour and a half. Dug her birth certificate out of her mother's lingerie drawer (funny thing about that—the space for father's name was left blank and Leila's birth was recorded with Pearl's maiden name) and took the bus to the main post office, where she enlisted in the Women's Army Auxiliary Corps.

I Wanted to See
Another Side of Life

Y ou did what? Did you lose your damn mind?"

Pearl Branch's voice nearly lifted the roof off the three-story Victorian Italianate. The volume was a shock to the tenant in #4, who was sleeping off the last evening's frivolity. And the profanity startled the railroad brakeman—who was, fortunately, not on third shift this week—from his daily Bible study. Perhaps the interruption was not a bad thing, as he was struggling with a tedious section from Genesis 36, which set out in excruciating detail the sons of this and the daughters of that. He thought that Pearl's choice of words was troubling, however.

"I joined the . . ."

Pearl slammed the rolling pin on the table and the dishes danced away as if there'd been an earthquake.

"I heard you the first time."

"Then why did . . ." The words disintegrated. Leila gulped. Her mother's eyes, luminous gold-green orbs when she was content, now glowed as if she was possessed by a demon.

"You can't join the army. You're underage, you're a child. *My* child." Pearl waved the kitchen towel to disperse the smoke from the second cigarette she'd lit in as many minutes. "You need my permission to join."

"No, I don't, Momma. I'm almost twenty."

Her mother glared at her. Leila might as well have said that she was forty-five.

"Well, you can just march down there and tell them that you made a mistake. I need you here."

Leila snorted, then bit her lip. Yes, she was nineteen, but that wouldn't stop Pearl Branch from disciplining her. Age was no excuse for disrespecting your mother. Pearl's malevolent gaze intensified. Leila inhaled deeply and decided to proceed anyway. *It's your funeral*, her conscience warned.

"No, you don't. I don't work here now, Momma, haven't for months. I'm at the Gibbons Hotel. 'Sides, you don't need me now that Isaac has moved in."

Ooo. Shouldn't have said that, Leila thought. Touchy subject, Isaac. Officially, he rented #6. Unofficially, he shared Pearl's bed and helped her with anything that she needed help with. But it was not a subject that Pearl was prepared to discuss with her daughter. In Pearl's mind, Leila was a child despite the fact that she had a child of her own.

"Humph. That's beside the point," Pearl barked back. "The point is, Miss I'm-All-Grown-Up-and-Joining-the-Army, you seem to have thought of everything. Everything except . . . who's going to take care of Paris, hmm? Did you think of that?"

Leila had to admit that, no, she hadn't, at least, not in any serious way. She had assumed, as she always did, that she could leave Paris with her mother and go. Now, she had to face the fact that while she'd had Paris in mind from the moment she'd heard "twenty-one dollars a month" plus "army" in the same sentence, her solution to what would happen to him while she was away was faulty. At least, it wasn't well thought out. She'd reacted just like a schoolgirl would. No plan, no forethought. A Bible verse flitted at the edge of her thoughts.

When I was a child, I spake as a child, I understood as a child, I thought as a child: but when I became a man, I put away childish things.

And now that I'm a woman and a mother, I, too, must put away childish things.

Leila felt as if she had been struck by lightning. Her mother's eyes were still shooting sparks and her lips were moving, but Leila didn't hear anything except the beating of her own heart. Leila *was* her mother's child but not a child anymore. She had a child of her own. A child whose life depended on *her*, not Pearl, not Mrs. Battle, not Isaac. Leila was Paris's mother. His father was . . . well, the less said about him the better. Leila was responsible for Paris, end of story. And now she'd gone off, without a word to anyone, and enlisted. The recruiter had told her to expect orders in a few weeks; he said she'd need to report to Ft. Hayes in Columbus and then would be shipped off to basic training from there. Leila hadn't given Paris's situation a moment's thought. And she should have. *She* was responsible for him.

Time to stop flying by the seat of your britches, girl. Grow up and get a plan. Grow up and take care of your son so that he'll have a life. That was why she had enlisted in the first place.

". . . you think you can just waltz in here and announce to me what you're going to do? I didn't raise you that way. I didn't . . ."

"Momma. I'm sorry. Really," Leila interrupted, as her thoughts and her mother's angry voice collided. "I didn't think it through the way I should have." Leila sighed.

"Humph" was Pearl's comment. "No, you damn sure didn't. And there's another thing . . ."

"I'm still joining the army, Momma," Leila said, her thoughts still in a fog. "I shoulda talked it over with you before I did it. I admit that. But let me explain. The only person I thought of was Paris. And you. But mostly Paris." She raised her gaze to the ceiling and pictured the image of her son now taking a nap in the bedroom above them. "The army is paying twenty-one dollars a month. Twenty-one dollars. They provide uniforms and necessities. And meals. I just thought . . . well, I'm young, I'm strong, and I'm a fast learner. I do what they tell me to do. I would be doing my part for the war effort. And they'll pay me. And I can earn more. That money can go to you. To help with this place." She gestured toward the ancient stove and the damp spots on the kitchen wall that needed paint. "And it would keep

Paris. Plus some. There would be money left to put aside for him. For clothes and shoes and . . . well, for Paris to have a life. A real life."

Pearl's mouth was open when Leila began speaking but was now closed. She slid a chair out from the table and sat down, stubbed her cigarette out in the ashtray. Listened. And remembered how she'd felt when she learned that she and her baby, Leila, were on their own.

"I know it's a lot to ask. He's a handful, Paris is. But if you could just keep him until I get . . . well, situated somewhere. Or whatever happens after I get my first assignment, then . . . well, maybe I could . . ." Leila stopped as her mother quietly lit another cigarette.

"Hush, girl. Let me tell you something." Pearl looked at her daughter. Her eyes had returned to their normal color. "I . . . well, Isaac and me, we're getting married in a month or so. I was waiting for the right moment to tell you. Isaac makes enough money for me to pull back a bit on taking in lodgers. So I'll be able to do some redecorating around this dump." She looked around her kitchen and smiled slightly. "Slap a couple coats of paint on Paris's room upstairs." She studied her daughter again. "I'll take care of Paris; of course I will. Isaac loves that boy as if he was his own. And we'll have enough between us that we won't have to dip into your twenty-one dollars." Pearl bit her lip then smiled and took another drag of her cigarette. "Well, maybe just a li'l bit."

Leila's eyes flooded and she hugged her mother.

"Thanks, Momma. Thanks so . . ."

"Baby girl, don't get all mushy on me!" Pearl barked, wiping her eyes with the back of one hard-water reddened hand. She took Leila's face between her palms and kissed her on the forehead. "I used to be a young momma, too, you know. And I wanted *my* baby to have the chance of some kind of life. Looks like you're taking the first step on your own. And it's a doozy!"

Uncle Sam (Doesn't) Want You

February 1943
Atlanta, Georgia

After the attack on Pearl Harbor, it wasn't difficult to join the army. Anybody could sign their life and freedom away in moments. Unless they were a Negro woman.

The sergeant or lieutenant—Dorothy wasn't sure about the ranks equating to the brass bars or the chevrons—stared. Dorothy waited. The man opened his mouth, but no sound came out. Dorothy cleared her throat. The man frowned. Dorothy fidgeted with the clasp on her handbag. *Oh, what the heck . . .*

Finally, the man spoke.

"The army isn't takin' any negra women."

Mercy.

"The army isn't takin' *negra* women." Dorothy's lip curled as she repeated the words a couple days later. She was sprawled across the sofa in Denie's front room. The appetizing aroma of coffee emanated from her aunt's cup, a dainty pink and ivory Limoges china confection that rested on a matching scallop-edged saucer.

"Well, clearly they are."

Denie was reading the latest edition of the *Atlanta Daily*, one of the city's Negro newspapers. She tapped a page with her finger. Only dark eyes and arched brows were visible above the top of the newspaper. Denie wore a pair of rhinestone-accented glasses that appeared more decorative than practical. "According to Mrs. Bethune." She might as well have said "according to God Almighty." Denie studied the page for another moment, then put the paper down and slid the glasses from her nose. "Off you go."

Dorothy rolled her eyes.

The clerk, whatever rank he held, the man who had rebuffed Dorothy on her first visit, was again on duty. Dorothy's heart sank. She was ready to give up on the whole thing.

"I'd like an application form please, sir," Dorothy said. "For the army." *Just to be clear.*

The man stared at her as he had before. Again, he didn't say anything. Dorothy stared back. The man seemed to be thinking—hard. A challenging algebraic equation, perhaps? Or maybe his bowels were giving him bother. Either way, Dorothy imagined that she could hear the gears turning in his brain and in his intestines.

Finally, he cleared his throat. And then he did something that surprised her. He retrieved a sheaf of papers from a file tray, extracted a couple pages, and affixed them to a clipboard, which he slid across the counter. Then he held out a pen.

"Fill these out and return them to me. I'll call your name when the lieutenant's ready for you."

Dorothy was so shocked that she nearly dropped the pen.

"Thank you."

The clerk-sergeant-whatever's expression was solemn but not hostile.

"You're welcome."

Dorothy discovered that it wasn't difficult to sign your life and freedom away to join the army once the forms were completed. All she had to do was sit and wait. Hours. Days. Wait until her name was called to take a physical. Wait before her name was called for a short interview to answer some questions. Then wait a bit more. The next time her name was called, she was asked, along with others who'd been sitting and waiting, to raise her right hand and swear allegiance to the United States of America. That was over in less than a quarter of the time that she'd spent waiting. *Congratulations, Miss Thom, now go home and wait some more.* But this time, her wait had a name. It was called a "furlough."

Her furlough wasn't spent in Atlanta, however, but in Cleveland, where her mother lived. Denie took her to the train station and Denie's former husband, Uncle George, went with them (without his new wife) to unload the cavernous trunk of his 1940 maroon Packard Custom Convertible, of which he was very proud.

George grunted as he struggled with Dorothy's large ivory-hued

suitcases—a going-away present from Denie, who said with authority that every lady should own a matching set of luggage.

"Dorothy! My goodness me!" he exclaimed, his Jamaican accent
adding grace notes to his words. "What have you in these luggage
here?" With a loud exhale, he set the cases down, pulled a snowy
white handkerchief from his inside coat pocket, and mopped his
broad forehead. "I cannot think you need all these t'ings at the
army barracks!"

His former wife snorted as she stepped by him to pick up
Dorothy's train case.

"George, it's not important what Dorothy has in the bags or
what you have . . ." Denie poked him lightly in his generous midsection. "There. Come on now. Let's get this child to the train."

Dorothy suppressed a giggle and fell in step with her aunt. It did
not surprise her that Denie had asked her former husband to drive
them to the station in his new automobile. Despite their turbulent
marriage, Uncle George was crazy about his strong-willed ex-wife
and would do most anything Denie would ask of him, including
marry her again, the new wife being a mere inconvenience.

"Uncle George has a point, Aunt Denie," Dorothy said as they
walked quickly toward the gates. "I can't imagine I'm going to
need . . . pillowcases, a hot-water bottle, blankets . . ." Her mind
jumped back to the serious packing that she and her aunt had done.
"All of these things!"

"You don't know what you'll need," her aunt interrupted. "The
fort where you're going . . . Ft. Dellroy . . ."

Dorothy chuckled. "Ft. Devens. Massachusetts."

"Right," continued Denie. "Ft. Whatchucallit. Out in the middle of nowhere. Best to have and not need than to need and not have."

Dorothy stopped and handed her small suitcase to the porter, who tipped his hat at her and blew a kiss to her aunt. "Speaking of . . . do you have a message that you want me to pass on to Mother? Best wishes perhaps? Love and a sisterly kiss?" Dorothy grinned. Denie and Eva were like oil and water.

Denie gave her the evil eye.

"No."

Uncle George finally caught up with them, handing off the bags and a few bills to the porter. Then he hugged his niece and slid a fat envelope into her hand.

"Goodbye, Dorothy, m'child. God bless you." He kissed her gently on the forehead.

"Thanks, Uncle."

Denie had stopped just to the side of the gate. Now she gave Dorothy the once-over appraisal, then kissed her on both cheeks. Dorothy felt the soft leather of her aunt's glove caress her cheek. Denie's dark eyes were wet but her lips curved upwards in a broad smile, her lipstick Elizabeth Arden Radiant Red. Dorothy had a brand-new tube of her own in her purse.

"That's how they do it in Paris. Both cheeks. Remember that when you go. And you will go, I'm sure of it. I love you, Little Dorothy."

The train horn sounded. Dorothy dabbed her eyes with a handkerchief and blew her nose. Denie grinned.

"Now, get on the darn train."

FURLOUGH

Spring 1943
On a train and other places

F urlough?" Leila remembered her mother saying as she read
the official letter that detailed Leila's orders and assignment.
It was just one of several mysterious words and phrases that populated the page. Some of them were so odd that Leila wondered if
they were English or some other language. Later, she would learn
that the military had its own dialect and vocabulary. Pearl stood on
her tiptoes in order to look over her daughter's shoulder. "What
the dickens is a furlough? Sounds like some kind of weird animal
with webbed feet. Like they got in Australia. Isaac showed me one
in the encyclopedia." Pearl sounded convinced.

Leila giggled.

"That's a platypus, Mom. A furlough is . . ." Leila paused because, well, she wasn't exactly sure *what* it was. The letter didn't spell it out, just said that Leila was to stay where she was for the next four weeks, then report to Ft. Hayes in Columbus for her physical and to be sworn in before being shipped out somewhere in Massachusetts for six weeks of basic training, whatever that was. Leila assumed that it had something to do with boots. She'd seen the photos in the newspapers.

"Humph," Pearl said. "Least they could do is tell you what you're s'posed to do with this furlough thing. Of course, since they don't say, I guess you can do what you want!"

"A furlough is an official leave of absence from duty, granted in most instances to a soldier."

When Leila Branch first met Dorothy Thom, she was in awe. A college graduate, a librarian, she had a voice like a real teacher and the mind to match. Not only that, Dorothy *knew* things. Unlike Leila, who in her own opinion knew absolutely nothing. Dorothy's "knowing" was like Christmas and a birthday rolled into one. But she didn't keep it to herself. She passed it around.

"You probably looked that up in the dictionary," Leila said, her fingers crossed behind her back.

Dorothy grinned.

"Yes, I did! What I know about military acronyms and terms would fit into a thimble! Of course I looked it up!"

And Leila, taking the hint and wanting to be the kind of mother that Paris would look up to, made a mental note to buy herself a dictionary once she got her first wage packet. And to look up the word "acronym."

They met in a makeshift dressing room at Ft. Hayes in Columbus. Along with twenty-three other women, Black and white, Dorothy and Leila had reported for "duty"—a word that they would in the coming weeks learn a good deal about—and began the process with a thorough physical exam.

"I already passed the physical exam," Dorothy had protested to the officer in charge.

"Not *this* physical exam," the officer said, grinning.

The women dressed and undressed, then dressed again; passed each other in the halls, going and coming; waited on hard wooden chairs for their turn with the doctors, chatting and napping; and were systematically poked, prodded, and bled—tested for this, tested for that. And once they were declared "fit for service," they were given orders to report to Ft. Devens, Massachusetts, *wherever* that was, for basic training, *whatever* that was. Not that it mattered to Leila, who'd never been anywhere.

Something about train travel lends itself to conversations, naps, staring out of windows (even when it's too dark to see anything), and the sharing of confidences. Train travel also teased out thoughtfulness and melancholy. The click-clack of the wheels along with the rocking motion brought out daydreams and the what-ifs. It brought out regrets, the why-didn't-I's. And for Leila, who had never been on a train before, who had never even been farther than Columbus, the train brought out excitement. And tears.

Once the dust settled from the confrontation with Pearl, the weeks of furlough passed quickly and were pleasant, quiet, and free of conflict. Leila was touched when her mother presented her with new underwear, socks, and other items that she thought would be useful and helped Leila pack. Isaac drove them from store to store, a luxury for Leila, who was accustomed to walking or taking the bus. Two nights before she left for Columbus, Pearl, Isaac, their neighbors, and friends threw a surprise going-away party. Pearl cooked all day, her uncles and aunts brought pies and cakes, and Isaac made sure that every glass was filled. Pearl's tenants, many of whom had known Leila since she was a girl, joined the festivities, including the Bible-studying Methodist brakeman who, although teetotal himself, contributed a bottle of his sister's dandelion wine.

It was wonderful, one of the best experiences Leila had ever had. She was too excited to eat, couldn't sleep as she imagined the unknown, letting dreams of the mysterious "army life" carry her away. She told herself that she was ready. A new life awaited her. And like the butterfly, Leila was ready to leave the cocoon behind.

She had forgotten one thing.

Pearl had dressed him in a navy blue outfit of jacket and shorts, and his high-top white shoes were immaculate. His wavy light brown hair was parted on the side and brushed smooth, his face scrubbed to an almost-shine, replacing the traces of milk or sticky jam that tended to reside there. Even his knees were clean—although Pearl had affixed a bandage to the left one, which was still healing from a scrape. He stood quietly beside his grandmother, as instructed, and looked solemnly at his mother.

"Bye, Mommy," he said, his little voice strong but high. His hazel eyes—a trait of Pearl's that had bypassed Leila—were wide and clear.

And when Leila took in the gravity of what she was about to do and her impending separation of unknown length from her son, she burst into tears and pulled the boy to her.

Oh my goodness, by the time I get back, he'll be all grown up.

She knew that was an exaggeration, but it was how she felt. Paris was two and a half. In three years, the projected term of her enlistment, he would be almost six.

"Oh, my baby . . ." Leila crooned as the sobs rocked them back and forth.

"Mommy, don't cry," Paris said, patting her cheek as he tried to wipe the tears away.

"Will you be a good boy for Grandma?" she asked, choking on the words. She squeezed her son, then released him, realizing that she was holding him too tightly.

Paris nodded.

"I be a good boy, Mommy."

I be a good boy.

The words rolled around in her head from that moment on. During the two-hour bus ride to Columbus. At night and in her dreams, Paris's round face and solemn expression invaded her dreams, his chubby hand patting her cheek. His words carefully said as he had been taught: "I be a good boy, Mommy." And for the twenty-hour train ride from Ohio to northwestern Massachusetts, she heard his voice and saw his face in her daydreams and her night dreams.

Why am I doing this? Why I am going away from my child for two, maybe even three years? I need my head examined.

So that he will have a life, she kept repeating to herself as she struggled to make herself comfortable in her train seat without disturbing Dorothy, who was slumbering in the seat across from hers.

So that he will have a life and his mother will too. Leila gave up and shook herself awake, wiping the tears from her cheek with the back of her hand. She looked out of the window into the darkness. This pain she felt in her stomach, a hollow, cold sensation, Leila realized that it was what she was supposed to feel. It was the consequence of taking responsibility. Of looking farther down the road and making decisions for her son's life and her own. It was the pain of being a mother.

*　　*　　*

"Dorothy?"

Her name, half spoken, half whispered. Her shoulder poked by a finger.

"Dorothy!"

Dorothy woke with a jerk, kicked out with her left foot, and stubbed her toe. The stab of pain caused her body to jerk in the opposite direction and she banged her elbow against the armrest. The funny-bone nerve sent a jolt up her arm that felt anything but funny.

"Owww!" Dorothy wailed. "Damn!"

A woman in the row in front of them shot a look of disapproval in Dorothy's direction.

Leila's expression was pained.

"I'm so sorry. I didn't mean to startle you," she said in a loud whisper, sinking into the seat across from Dorothy's. Leila patted her arm. "You must have been having a bad dream. You called out a few times." Leila suppressed a smile. "And you were snoring."

Dorothy was mortified.

"I'm sorry too. I didn't realize that I was asleep." She yawned. Leila passed over a glass of water.

"It's okay. I just wanted to check . . . that you weren't having a fit or something."

Dorothy took a sip and smiled.

"No. No fits." She yawned again. She felt exhausted. "I'm fine. You were right. It was just a bad dream."

About my mother.

Dorothy's new army "mate" settled back into her seat. This time it was Leila who yawned. She fluffed up her small travel pillow and burrowed into it.

Dorothy stared out into the darkness of . . . Pennsylvania? Or were they now in New York? Yes, Dorothy thought, train travel did encourage the sharing of confidences. But the family dynamics that worked Dorothy's nerves during her furlough in Cleveland with her mother, aunts, and uncles would need a friendship held together by stronger scaffolding than the few days that she and Leila had known each other.

Dorothy had asked her mother for quiet time and no fuss. What she got was shopping, excursions, fittings (no ready-made garment ever met Eva's standards), social events, church on Sunday, cocktails and night clubs on Friday and Saturday nights, and rounds of family visits. The days became a blur of to-ing and fro-ing. And opinions about what Dorothy should or should not be doing.

"Women don't belong in the army," Uncle Ed opined between puffs on his pipe. "I should know. I was in the dubya-dubya one war, the Great War. There's no place for women in a war. Unless

they nurses." *Puff, puff.* "And you aren't a nurse, Dorothy Mae."
Puff. "Now, when I was situated in Panama digging the canal . . ."

Lord have mercy.

Somehow Dorothy managed not to roll her eyes. Her middle
name was "Eugenia," not "Mae." And if she heard Uncle's story
about digging "the canal" one more time . . . Every detail of
Uncle's service in Panama had stayed with him: the heat, his com-
rades, the insects, and backbreaking work, it was all still vivid in
his mind. But while that was understandable, his story expanded
with each telling. Uncle Ed sometimes told different stories of his
war and *his* canal several times in an afternoon depending on the
situation or the audience.

"Weren't any gals there digging my canal," he added, lighting
another match and touching the bowl of his pipe. *Puff.*

Aunt Pat gave him an "Oh, shut up!" look and turned her attention to Dorothy.

"But what will you girls do in the army, Dorothy? As Eddie
says, it's not as if you all are nurses." She paused as a less accept-
able option entered her head. "Don't tell me that the army will use
you as maids!"

Uncle Ed choked on the smoke.

"Pat, you don't know what you talking about! They ain't no
maids in the army!" He puffed. "Though now I think on it, when I
was building my canal, there was a colonel who . . ."

Oh, for the love of heaven.

On Sunday, Eva made sure that Dorothy was the center of attention, introducing her to everyone within arm's reach—her
daughter who had joined the new Women's Army Auxiliary Corps.

"Mother! It's not like I'm the only one," Dorothy said, feeling self-conscious. "We aren't that special."

Eva snorted.

"You are if I say you are. You girls are Mrs. Bethune's special project. That makes you special. I'm not in favor of this . . . venture that you've taken on yourself. But we're going to treat it as if it's the greatest thing in the world. In my opinion, your aunt should've . . . well, Denie is what she is."

Dorothy felt a flash of anger. "Aunt Denie took us in and took care of us," she hissed. "She didn't have to do that."

Eva's jaw tightened.

"She did what I asked her to do," Eva barked, her blue eyes igniting like flashes of lightning. "And that's none of your business. You girls were children."

"Mom . . ."

"Fern! How are you, honey? Have you met my daughter? My baby girl? Dorothy dear, this is Mrs. Mills, Frances Mills. Fern, this is my daughter, Dorothy. She's staying with me for a few days to get some rest before she goes to Massachusetts to join Mrs. Bethune's group. You know, the Women's Army Auxiliary Corps?"

Dorothy smiled at the ecstatic Mrs. Mills, extended her hand, and recited a short prayer to herself.

Lord, I give thanks to you for the gifts of patience and good humor. And for the flask of gin in my train case. Amen.

THE GOOD LIFE

Spring 1943
Ft. Devens, Massachusetts

The weather was vile, stormy, and unsettling. When it rains in early April in northwestern Massachusetts near the New Hampshire state line, it's chilly, so just plan on being damp and cold. *And miserable*, Dorothy grumbled to herself. Because you're sitting on what amounts to a rough-hewn wooden bench in a cavernous and noisy army truck, scrunched elbow to elbow with your soon-to-be-WAC sisters bouncing down what feels like (because you can't see a darned thing in the late afternoon gloom) a rough pothole-marked road toward an army base named after a hometown boy who distinguished himself in the Civil War. A real in-the-middle-of-nowhere place, or so it seemed to Dorothy.

And she was cold, freezing. Dorothy was more acclimated to the humid warmth of Georgia and Florida. Her teeth were chattering. She might as well have not been wearing a wool coat for all the good it did. Even with gloves on, her fingertips were numb. And although she'd worn what she'd thought were her sturdiest walking shoes—handsome auburn leather brogues—as well as socks, her toes . . . What toes? She couldn't feel them anymore. She and Leila huddled together as close as they could, wincing with every sideways bounce of the truck as it lumbered along—they were sitting against one of the back tire wells—chatting nonstop about any and all subjects, inane and otherwise, whatever topic would take their mind's attention away from the misery. Which is why Dorothy chattered on about the history of their destination.

". . . his n-name was B-B-Brevet Major General Charles D-Devens," Dorothy managed to spit out, gulping a breath of air, which she hoped would settle her stomach. It was bad enough being cold but seasick? The truck's motion was worse than the rolling of a ship, or so she imagined. "B-But when it was first constructed on the site, it was mainly a training camp for troops going overseas in World War I. It was just plain 'Camp Devens' then."

Leila's complexion was the color of chalk.

"I can't believe you know all this stuff." Leila closed her eyes and exhaled laboriously. Then she smiled slightly. "What's a 'brevet'?"

As Dorothy recited the answer—a commission giving a military officer higher rank than he or she is paid for—Leila chuckled, and this time, dimples appeared in her pale cheeks.

"What?" Dorothy asked.

"Doro, how do you know this? What did you do, look it up in

the . . ." If there had been light in the cavernous transport, Leila would have seen Dorothy's cheeks reddening. "No. You actually looked it up?"

"I'm a librarian! It's my job to look things up!"

"Did you pack a set of encyclopedias?" This time there were giggles from both women.

Leila's laughter blended with the next clap of thunder. Startled, the two women jumped.

"No wonder your suitcase is so heavy. Those books weigh more than you do!"

They didn't, Dorothy reflected. Not quite. She'd brought a general reference book and a pocket-size dictionary. They distracted her from worrying about whether she had finally gotten herself into more adventure than she could handle. Looking words up, as she had told Leila, was a librarian's habit that distracted her from contemplating otherwise.

Ft. Devens was located some twenty miles from the New Hampshire border, fifty from Boston. The land's guardians were the Wampanoag people before this part of the country began its colonial history as an English fort in the 1650s. During the Civil War, it became "Camp Stevens" but was renamed and built up in 1917 to support a training camp during World War I. Then, in 1940, the camp was built up again—quickly—with the addition of two hospitals, an airfield, and scores of wooden buildings for use as barracks—it morphed into Ft. Devens. And now it served as a reception area for men and women, as well as a POW camp for German and Italian combatants.

Leila squeezed her arm.

"Doro, there's no one like you."

"My sisters called me 'Miss Know-It-All,'" Dorothy said glumly.

Leila's laughter was full-throated and warm despite the lack of color in her face.

"I will call you *Private* Know-It-All!"

Dorothy closed her eyes and swallowed. The truck had lurched again as its tires rolled into a pothole that felt as if it was the size of Rhode Island. Then it stopped abruptly and made an unsettling groan as it rocked forward, then back. They were stuck.

An earsplitting grinding of metal against metal put a halt to their conversation and those of their sister recruits. The grinding continued as the driver moved through the gears. The women were silent. The engine protested, sputtering as if searching for the energy to propel itself out of the ditch and back onto the road. The driver made another attempt—and again the gears complained. He waited a beat, then tried once more. On this try, finally, the engine picked up momentum and purred, then abruptly propelled the truck and its passengers forward.

Dorothy, Leila, and most of the other recruits tumbled into each other or onto the floor. As the truck picked up speed, the women cheered. Dorothy was so relieved that she forgot to be sick.

It was gloomy and spitting rain when they arrived in late afternoon, but a warm amber glow of light flooded through the windows of the reception center. It looked welcoming despite the damp chill in the air and the dreary charcoal-colored sky.

"Mind the steps," the driver chirped. He looked at Dorothy and grinned. "It's a long way down, little lady."

Oh, for goodness sake, I'm not that short! It isn't the bloody Grand Canyon!

And to make the point, she jumped.

And landed in a puddle. Her new brogues and the hem of her skirt were splattered with mud. Leila's laughter floated over her shoulder.

Through the open door of the reception center, a soldier was silhouetted against the bright light. As he stepped out of the glare, his broad smile and the clipboard he held came into view.

"Hello, ladies! Did you have a nice trip?" The tone of his voice was cheerful and many of the women responded in kind. "Let's get you inside out of this rain." He made a mark on his paper, then gestured to the left. "Now, will all the colored girls move over to this side?"

From behind her, Dorothy heard one of the women say, sotto voce, "Welcome to Ft. Devens, ladies. We may be in the army now, but we're still in the US of A."

*   *   *

Leila met lots of WAC recruits on the train ride from Columbus to Massachusetts and on the short but jarring truck bounce from the train station to Ft. Devens. Colored and white, they had a litany of reasons for joining up.

"I want to do my part."

"My husband's in the service and we don't have children. I figured that maybe I could help too."

"The money."

"Maybe I'll meet my (next) husband!"

"I felt stuck."

"To be exposed to another side of life."

"Well, we're certainly getting that!" This came from Dorothy who was definitely not having fun as she cleaned the mud from her once-beautiful leather shoes.

It was a lot to get used to. There was no expectation of privacy in a barracks of forty women. Time management meant that the army was managing your time. Fall out at five in the morning, reveille at six, parade formation, fall out, fall in, and classes from eight until five. Calisthenics, map reading, military courtesy ("Courtesy? Are they kidding?" Edna Lucas, a waitress from Tennessee, blurted out before being shushed by a giggling Leila), current events, poison-gas identification, and parade formation. And in their spare time, there were chores. Floors to mop, windows to clean, latrines ("They're shitters," grumbled the eloquent Edna again. "Call 'em what they are."), trash to collect, grounds to police. Not to mention KP duty.

After the first few weeks of basic training, regardless of their reasons for enlisting, the women—including soon-to-be privates Leila Branch and Dorothy Thom—all had the same comments—and complaints. Up at dawn (it's cold!), dress in the dark, tidy up, fall in, march, fall out, eat. Fall in, march, fall out, class. Salute sergeant here ("We don't have to salute the sergeant," Leila whispered. "Do we?"), salute bread delivery man there ("If it moves, salute it!" Dorothy whispered back), fall in, fall out, eat, march, class . . . It became a blur, along with a profusion of aches, pains, and sniffles to go with the hefty portions of whining.

"I don't think I've ever been so tired, cold, *and* hungry in my life." Dorothy was stretched out on her bed. Every muscle in her body ached. Glancing at her watch, she sighed. A half hour until supper. She wriggled her toes to satisfy herself that they were still attached. "All I wanted was a little adventure."

Leila, who normally looked on the bright side of every situation, nodded in agreement. She sat on the edge of the bed next to Dorothy's, elbows on her knees, her head in her hands, and a disappointed expression on her face.

"I just wanted to live 'the good life.'"

"Good life?" Dorothy snorted. "Oh, you'll get the good life eventually. But you'll be too tired to enjoy it! All I want for Christmas is for my uniforms to fit!" Dorothy held up one leg with its triple-cuffed hem. "Is that too much to ask?" she grumbled.

The army-issue skirts and trousers were made for someone a full four inches taller—Dorothy was altering them herself and it was tedious, time-consuming work. Her army-issue coat, with its thick double lining that blocked the cold wind blowing through Massachusetts from the Atlantic, was a man's coat—the service had finally begun distribution of military coats for its female recruits but there were more women than coats. Dorothy had to make do with a behemoth that was constructed for a man eight inches taller and fifty pounds heavier than she was. She tacked up the sleeves, but the hem was a challenge. She sighed. It dragged a bit but at least it kept her warm.

Leila shook her head.

"Yes, it is. But even that pales over the drills, and early mornings." She winced. She'd been rubbing a sore place on her heel. Dorothy knew that Leila was thinking about the loud, persistent reveille at six o'clock. Leila was not a morning person. ". . . and the food. I'm going to volunteer for kitchen duty. The scrambled eggs are disgusting. Even I could do better than that! And I don't cook!" Another wince. "When does the adventure part begin?"

Dorothy massaged her upper arm, still tender from the retinue of shots she'd been given: typhoid, tetanus, smallpox.

"An hour after the marching," she quipped. "Line up! Hut! One, two! Keep up! Move it, soldiers! Thom, think you can march? I don't think so! Keep up, Branch!" She groaned and massaged her shoulder. "I've saluted every man, woman, squirrel, and coat rack on this base!"

"I am not used to getting yelled at all the time!" Leila said slowly. Dorothy felt a pang of sympathy for her friend. Leila had, by simply breathing, attracted the enmity of the sergeant in charge, who berated her every move. It seemed as if she could not do anything right.

"Well, I can do you one better," she told her friend. "I'm the youngest of three girls and both of my sisters were goody-two-shoes and tattletales. I was yelled at a lot. It was: 'Quit! Stop that! What do you think you're doing?' And 'Dorothy, what were you thinking?'" Dorothy shrugged. "Still is, in fact."

Leila grinned.

"So I should treasure the joys of being an only child," she mused. Shivering, she rubbed her arms. "It's drafty in here. The only place I get warm these days is in bed." She gazed enviously at the thick oatmeal-colored blanket that was folded neatly and arranged on top of the chest at the foot of Dorothy's bed.

"You're a genius, Doro, bringing along that wool blanket."

Leila spoke each word deliberately, pausing in between to sigh as if she was talking about a piece of rich chocolate candy. "It's so cozy looking that it's delicious."

Dorothy smiled. She wished Denie was here to listen. Her aunt had insisted on packing the blanket, a hot-water bottle, four pairs of extra-thick socks, and other items that had added so much weight to Dorothy's suitcase (when combined with the weight of the dictionary) that she needed two trips to the reception area to carry her things to the barracks.

Dorothy smoothed the blanket with the palm of her hand. "God bless Aunt Denie," she said, and meant it. "She told me, and I quote, 'It's better to have and not need than to need and not have.'"

"The woman's a prophet," Leila commented. "And when you're not looking, I plan to swipe that blanket!"

"Attention!"

A mad scramble ensued. The NCO in charge of their unit, Sergeant Banks, watched the mayhem without expression. Then he cleared his throat and proceeded.

"Er . . . ladies. The CO, Lieutenant Colonel Havers, arrives on post tonight and will perform inspection on these premises at 0900 tomorrow. I expect you to look sharp and have these barracks . . ." His visual survey was performed without a smile of satisfaction. "Shipshape for the colonel. Is that understood?"

"Yes, sir, Sergeant Banks, sir!"

"As you were!"

The murmurs began the moment the sergeant left the barracks. Leila leaned close to Dorothy, her eyes wide.

"So. What are we supposed to do for an inspection?"

INSPECTION

After supper, there was a frenzy of activity as the women swept, mopped, wiped, folded, organized, and polished. They closed cabinets, packed trunks near to bursting, and secured the fasteners. Leila had to sit on Dorothy's so that it would close properly, prompting another woman to take her place because, as she put it, "That gal doesn't have enough lead in her ass!" They ironed curtains and cleaned the windows until they shone. When that was finished, with barely half an hour remaining before lights out at ten, a swarm of women gathered around Private Dorothy Thom's bed for a tutorial on bed making.

"Got it?" Dorothy looked up and noted that several of the women nodded in agreement. "Okay. And before you move to the other side, run your palm down the side of the bed to make sure that the sheet is smooth, no lumps. Then take this corner and tuck it under, just so, making a right angle." Some of the women took notes.

"Thom, you should be in charge of bed making, period," said Edna. "You explain it better than Sergeant Banks."

"She's fast too. Look at that," Roberta "Bobbie" Norman commented. "That gal could make up five beds in the time it takes me to make one!"

"Where'd you learn to do that, Doro?" asked Bettie Corbett, a twenty-year-old secretary from Louisville.

"Mercy! Didn't your mommas teach you anything?!" Dorothy teased. Her remark brought protests and recriminations from some of her sister recruits.

"My mother didn't want me to do housework," Bettie responded defensively. "She said she wasn't raising me up to be anybody's maid."

"I can fix up a bed," Edna fired back. "Just not like that," she conceded.

"Uh-huh . . ." Dorothy commented as she whipped another corner of the bed into shape. Dorothy used her fingers to "press" it into a sharp crease before tucking it down and under the mattress. "Attention!"

"Give us a break, Thom," Leila commented, a wide grin lighting up her face. "And tell us the truth. Where'd you learn to make a bed like that? Military style. As far as I know, you haven't been in the army before."

Dorothy shook her head and grinned.

"No, I haven't. And this isn't military style, this is Aunt Emmie style." She smoothed out an imaginary wrinkle with her palm. "But it ought to get us through this inspection."

Leila rolled her eyes.

"Oh, lordy. Another one of this girl's amazing aunts."

There were murmurs of approval from the women who were watching. Many of them had "Aunt Emmies" in the family too.

"She's a practical nurse. She can make a bed that you can bounce a quarter on."

"If I had a quarter," commented one of the women standing in the back. Laughter followed this remark.

"This is a hospital bed, ladies," Dorothy instructed, raising her voice slightly so that the women in the back could hear. "But perhaps close enough to the military way of bed making. Not that anyone's actually *showed* us the military way of bed making. But think about it. We all know those generals didn't start out at West Point knowing how to make a bed!"

"Course not!" Edna said, with a small edge of bitterness. "They had mothers, wives, or colored maids to make their beds!"

More laughter followed and then applause as Dorothy finished the task, smoothing the khaki-green blanket that completed the process.

"Where's your heavy wool blanket?" Leila whispered with a mischievous grin on her face. "The one that your aunt packed."

Dorothy held a finger against her lips.

"Out of sight, out of mind. I'll use my coat if I get cold. It comes down to my ankles so it ought to keep me warm enough."

The next morning, at 0900 sharp, the forty women of barracks #4 lined up and stood at attention in anticipation of the arrival of the CO. They were dressed in their work uniforms, khaki shirts and pants, boots and hats at hand, alert and ready. The women's faces were scrubbed; their hair was neatly pinned above their collars per regulation. Their fatigues were ironed to near perfection, not a wrinkle to be seen. On their feet were the rigid army-issue black leather boots, a misery to wear since the quartermaster hadn't yet obtained a broad enough array of sizes to accommodate all of the women's feet. Dorothy's boots were a size too large so she stuffed socks into the toes, which made her walk like she had a stick up her butt. The left one worried the bunion on her big toe. Plus the khaki trousers were starched so heavily (Bobbie ironed Dorothy's khakis as payment for the bed-making tutorial but had gotten carried away) that the fabric made her itch. But scratching was a temptation that she would have to resist when standing at attention under the commanding officer's scrutiny.

By 0915, Sergeant Banks notified the women that the CO was on his way. So Edna hastily stubbed out a barely consumed Lucky Strike. By 0930, there was no CO and no further word from Sergeant Banks. Barracks #4 was vibrating with grumbles and complaints about sore feet and aching backs. By 1045, with neither CO nor sergeant in sight or in transit, the women of barracks #4 were in elevated "as you were" mode. Edna was on her third cigarette, a woman named "Lou" who was from Cape Girardeau had removed her wig, and Dorothy was sitting on her bed, rubbing ointment on her throbbing toe, the offending boot lying on its side under another recruit's bed where she had thrown it in a fit of temper. A few of the women were in the toilets; another pair was playing cards; and Leila, who was suffering with a head cold, had stretched out on her bunk to take a catnap.

"Attention!"

"Damn."

The ensuing scramble resembled the iconic scene from the Marx Brothers film *A Night at the Opera*. It was so chaotic that both sergeant and colonel didn't know where to look. The cacophony was earsplitting.

Women appeared from every direction to fall in—not at the same time but close enough—and in every imaginable state of dress or undress. Lou's wig found its way onto her head but it was lopsided. Leila couldn't stop sneezing as she pulled herself into a form of "attention." Dorothy was standing in line in front of her bed, with one boot on and one boot off. She hadn't had time to grab the other one from beneath Ann's bed. There was a flurry of activity as they tucked shirts in, smoothed hair, zipped trousers, and in one case, buttoned an open shirt.

The men's expressions morphed from startled and embarrassed to somber as they exchanged glances. After the brief uproar, the barracks settled into silence except for the muffled sound of a flushing toilet. A few minutes passed, which seemed longer to the men than it did to the women, before the sergeant officially called the women to attention—again—and the formal inspection began.

Every item in barracks #4 was examined, and that included the women. Beds, trunks, cabinets. Windows and doors, toilets and sinks. The colonel had a particular interest in the immaculate state of the floors, prompting someone to mutter under her breath, "Name me one Negro woman who can't mop a floor." Sergeant Banks pretended not to hear and walked on. The colonel mentioned several deficits to the sergeant, none of which were notable, and while noting the various states of dress or undress, declined to cite the women, much to Banks's relief, since it was, as Lt. Colonel Havers said, "their first inspection."

Finally, the women saluted and the CO left.

"At ease, men, er, ladies," Banks barked out before following behind the commanding officer and closing the door. "Well done."

The two men were well down the path toward the mess hall when the sound of riotous laughter reached their ears.

The women of barracks #4 celebrated. They had passed their first official inspection. That in itself was impressive since, as Sergeant Banks reflected later to one of his buddies over a beer, no one—not even he—had thought to instruct the women on exactly what they were supposed to *do* for an inspection.

FT. DES MOINES

They learned fast. Boot camp, basic training, hell, whatever you wanted to call it, the process of transforming a civilian, whether farm laborer, waitress, teacher, or maid into a soldier—from the inside out and the top of the head to the soles of the feet—was a business that the military took seriously. It was a transformation that required longer than six weeks. But the US Army had a war on and six weeks was all the time allowed. There were procedures to learn, lingo to memorize, duties to perform, and a hierarchy to respect. There were more do's and don'ts to obey. The wardrobe, if fatigues and "arctics" could be called that, replaced dresses, Sunday hats, and high-heeled pumps. And in changing the outward woman, the rough khakis and black boots simultaneously changed the woman inside.

It was just so different. Take what you knew about civilian or "reg'lar" life, as one of the women called it, turn it on its head, and *that* was army life. The clothes, the language ("Yes, it's a mess all right," Edna grumbled during dinner one night), the accommodations ("This is not a hotel, Branch," the sergeant reminded Leila), even the air they breathed was different. It took Dorothy some time before she could relax and fall asleep surrounded by so many women. She'd shared a bedroom with her sisters, and even though Hattie snored, that was nothing when compared to the rows and rows of beds in the barracks, each one occupied by a breathing woman. Exhaustion was the only sleep aid, a nod to the demanding daily schedule and its sunrise to sunset work details. The communal showers and toilets were another challenge. Dorothy didn't think she would ever adjust to them. Privacy was worth its weight in gold, silver, and precious stones. Like the lost city of El Dorado, it was legendary and impossible to find. Wearing khakis and boots, Dorothy had become a barking, marching, and saluting machine. Would she ever be herself again?

As the weeks progressed and the women stood at attention in neat rows, day after day, rain or shine, the metamorphosis began to take hold. And on a cloudy, cool day in June 1943, the women of barracks #4 and their sister recruits lined up in formation on the Ft. Devens parade grounds and accepted their promotions. Less than a week later, Pvt. Dorothy Thom and Pvt. Leila Branch received orders to report to the Administration School at Ft. Des Moines, Iowa, for the next phase of their training.

The train ride took over thirty-six hours. For most of that time, Dorothy barely slept. Like a child, she was so excited that she couldn't sit still, much less sleep. It wasn't the passing landscape that kept her awake. Passing through Ohio, Indiana, and Illinois, the flat farmland vistas gave way to prairie dull enough to put anyone to sleep. Hazel and Rainey snoozed in the seats across from her. Beside her, Leila snored. But not Dorothy. She had never been this far away from home before and she didn't want to miss a thing, even if Iowa was flatter than a pancake. Finally! Her adventure was about to begin. Dorothy was all about what interesting experience happened next.

She tried to write a letter to Aunt Denie, but after five attempts and as many sheets of notepaper, she gave up. She only managed a few words beyond *Dear Aunt Denie, How are you all? I am doing fine.* Dorothy looked over at Leila and adjusted the scratchy army-issue green blanket that had slipped from her shoulders. Leila was all about sending home her next paycheck.

Since the US entered the war in December 1941, Ft. Des Moines, like many other American military posts, was in a dynamic construction phase, expanding its facilities and adding personnel to keep pace with the intense war effort. The former frontier cavalry post, last overhauled during World War I, had outgrown its original premises—the horses were long gone, replaced by jeeps and lumbering supply trucks—and a "boomtown" rose up on newly annexed land. The newest buildings weren't finished yet—there were no sidewalks in some places—so in order to keep up with the training and processing of new recruits, many of them women, Ft. Des Moines's CO requisitioned office buildings and hotels in downtown Des Moines. And so it was that Dorothy, Leila, and a contingent of women from Ft. Devens found themselves temporarily housed in the Chamberlain Hotel.

The four women assigned to the tenth floor double room surveyed their new quarters. Each wore an expression of dismay.

"*This* is a double room?" Lorraine "Rainey" Barbour, a North Carolina native, was incredulous. She tapped the wall with one fingertip. "Okay."

Hazel Diggs raised one elegant eyebrow, then stepped into the bathroom. The Kansas City born music teacher was a classically trained singer, pianist, and eloquent orator. Her assessment of her new room assignment was not eloquent.

"This is foolishness! A double room? This room isn't a double anything! Two people can get in here. Maybe. If one of 'em is two feet tall!"

"That even leaves you out, Dorothy," Rainey quipped.

"It might have been the thing once," Leila said in a flat voice, looking around the bare-bones double room. "It sure isn't now." She dropped her duffel on an unfolded newspaper that Dorothy had thoughtfully spread across the lower bunk. "But next to Ft. D, it ain't half bad."

"Never put your handbag or your luggage on the floor," Doro had told her when they first met at Ft. Hayes.

"The only things luxurious in this room are the draperies," Hazel commented, running her hand down a smooth satin-like ivory fabric. "Otherwise . . ." Her voice trailed off.

The once-posh Chamberlain Hotel was now an army barracks—all twelve floors of it—and its spacious accommodations, highly prized before the war, had been taken over for the war effort. Transitioned to a women's barracks, each guest room was furnished with two sets of bunk beds in each, one bathroom, barely large enough for Dorothy, at five feet, one inch, to turn around in. A coin toss took place to decide which woman slept in the top bunk and which in the bottom.

Dorothy groaned. *Tails.*

"Shouldn't the short person get the lower bunk?" she asked hopefully.

Leila's laughter was her answer.

"I'm willing to pay," Dorothy said, unzipping her duffel bag. "In order to take the lower bunk."

Leila rolled her eyes.

"No way."

"At least think about it," Dorothy added, grinning as she held up four rolls of toilet paper, then waved them with a triumphant flourish.

Leila sighed. Now it was Rainey's turn to laugh.

"Doro, we were allotted two rolls each," she said with an expression of surprise on her face. "How did you end up with four?" Toilet paper was meticulously rationed—two rolls per woman per month (or so) but no definite word on when the next allotment was due.

"The better to bribe me with," Leila said glumly, moving her pillow from the lower bunk to the top one.

"Thank you, baby girl," Dorothy said with exaggerated sweetness. "And thank you, Aunt Denie! Again!"

As Ft. Des Moines continued its evolution into what would become known as the "West Point for women," the Chamberlain's dining room and its dramatic interior design was transformed into a mess, the induction center took over the lobby, and the expansive salons became classrooms. Classes ran from 8:00 a.m. to 4:00 p.m., then dinner, two hours for study, and lights out at 10:00 p.m. Even in college, Dorothy hadn't taken courses as mind-numbing as what passed for "Administration 101" at Admin School. Because of the urban location, marching was at a minimum and only possible on the vast lawn in front of the capitol building. So when the school day ended, the women fell into formation and marched up the many flights of stairs to their respective quarters—it would've taken too long for the elevators to transport them all. For Dorothy, Leila, and their mates, this meant the tenth floor. The army, struggling to maintain segregation despite its obvious inconvenience and expense, assigned the white WACs to the lower floors and the Negro WACs to the upper ones.

"There's only one good thing about this death march," Dorothy grumbled on that afternoon as she and her roommates huffed and puffed up to the next-to-last stairwell before reaching the tenth floor.

"I can't think of one darned thing," Rainey muttered, breathing heavily. "My calves are burning!"

Dorothy giggled.

"Mine are too. But the good thing is, we're walking off the weight we've gained from eating all those hot fudge sundaes!"

Their laughter echoed as it bounced against the walls of the cavernous stairwells.

"Des Moines isn't New York," Rainey commented.

"Or Dayton," Leila said.

"Or Atlanta. Mercy!" exclaimed Dorothy.

"Or Kansas City," Hazel agreed.

No "white only" signs, no "colored" drinking fountains, but surly service in the downtown department stores and confusion in local restaurants, including at a soda fountain in the drugstore across the street from the hotel, was a regular occurrence.

"As if they never seen Negroes before," Rainey noted.

"Negroes in uniform," Dorothy added.

"The best hot fudge sundae I've ever tasted!" Betsy Sizemore crooned with a sigh, then rolled her eyes. "Whipped cream on top. Mountains of it." She sighed again. "Well . . ." Betsy was a white girl from eastern Kentucky, so her one syllable words usually stretched into two. "It's better than sex!"

Gasps, giggles, heads shaking, and a chorus of "Betts!" greeted her remarks from across the table. Dorothy pretended to cover Leila's ears.

"Yes, I'm young," Leila said, laughing. "But I have a three-year-old and he wasn't dropped off by a stork!"

"You all need to go there," Betsy said, talking and chewing her roll at the same time.

The women of room 1020—Dorothy, Leila, Hazel, and Rainey—were in the mess, formerly the hotel dining room, eating dinner with the women of room 605, Betsy and another WAC from West Virginia plus one from Wisconsin and one from Maine. The army had tried and failed to implement lasting segregation in the mess because the women, who spent their days in integrated classrooms, decided on their own it was a useless exercise and sat where they pleased. Integrating the lunch counter at the Walgreens drugstore across the street, however, was bound to be a different matter.

Pfc. Betsy Sizemore crooned that the ice cream sundaes were legendary. Rich freshly churned vanilla ice cream; chocolate syrup so rich and thick that Betts called it "liquid fudge"; crushed nuts and mountains of whipped cream arranged in a soft white tower of "yumminess," a comment contributed by Patience Penn, a private from a small town in Maine with an unpronounceable name.

"That's not a word, P," Dorothy commented using her best schoolteacher tone, her mouth watering, thinking that a mountain of whipped cream would suit her just fine.

Patience shrugged.

"It is now."

"And the root beer floats . . ." Betts continued in a dreamy voice.

To hear Patience tell it, they were "epic" and the milkshakes (so thick that the straws barely moved) were "to die for."

"That's it. I want a milkshake," Dorothy said, "to go with the whipped cream. I don't care if it does go straight to my thighs."

"A sundae for me," Leila chimed in. "No. Root beer float."

"Two scoops of chocolate ice cream," Patience interjected. "'S all I want. Two gigantic scoops."

"The question is," Hazel cut in, "can we sit at the counter or in a booth? Or do we have to eat outside, standing on the sidewalk?" She glanced in Betts's direction.

Betts's eyes widened.

"I . . . don't know. I didn't notice . . ."

The private from Maine frowned.

"Why would you have to eat standing on the sidewalk?"

Five pairs of eyes—belonging to the WAC resident in room 1020 and Betts—turned in Patience's direction.

"Right. Okay. I didn't think that . . . um . . . I guess I just didn't realize . . ." Patience bit her lip. "I know this is going to sound strange but . . . there are no Negroes living in Whycocomagh, Maine."

Leila smiled.

"That's because nobody can pronounce it."

Dorothy stood up, grabbing her tray.

"Well, I'm in the mood for a strawberry milkshake. Who's going to join me?"

*   *   *

It was standing room only. Customers were lined up in the aisles, on the sidewalk, and shoulder to shoulder at the counter. The noise was deafening: music, conversation, laughter, shouts, hands rose in greetings.

"And this is only Wednesday night . . ." Patience yelled.

Dorothy, who was standing one person away, cupped her hand around her ear.

"I didn't hear you! What?"

"I said . . ." Patience, who'd gotten separated from the other women, smiled at the man in front of her, then elbowed her way past him toward Dorothy. "I said . . . it's only Wednesday. Imagine what this place is like on the weekend."

Dorothy nodded.

"I wonder how long it will take to get served."

"Help you gals?" The soda jockey grinned at Patience, whose russet-colored hair, which had escaped from its neat bun beneath her Hobby cap, always attracted attention.

"Can we get a booth?" Patience, taller than the rest of the women, stood on her tiptoes. "I don't see any room at the counter."

The soda jockey shook his head.

"We're jammed, no joke. I'll take your orders here. By the time they're ready, there'll prob'ly be room. How many of you?"

Patience gestured toward Betts, Dorothy, Leila, and Hazel. A slight frown appeared on the boy's face.

"Oh. I don't know if . . ."

Dorothy beamed. Her smile radiated warmth and the dimples in her cheeks were irresistible. But it was more devious than it seemed. Dorothy called it her "Aunt Denie smile."

"Come on, hon," she said in a slow Georgia drawl with just enough honey and peach preserves dripping over every syllable. It was a miracle that he could even hear her over the noise. "Go'on and take our orders. We'll stand right here and wait." She blew him a kiss.

"I don't know if I'm gonna wait long," Hazel grumbled, stepping out of one of her heels. "This bunion is giving me the blues."

"Take a seat," Leila said, pointing to an empty stool to her right. Her eyes widened. "Margo's got a seat."

"Where?" Dorothy asked, standing on her tiptoes to get a better view.

"To your left. At the far end of the counter."

The women followed Leila's directions. Sure enough, Margo

and what appeared to be a chocolate shake were parked at the south end of the counter.

Hazel didn't say anything, but her eyes flickered with amusement. The soda fountain was packed with people, military and civilian, women and men, Negro and white. But only the white people were seated. Until now. Hazel didn't waste a moment and was soon comfortably seated on the round maroon cushion. The soda jockey's eyes bulged.

"Um. Ah . . ."

"I'll have two scoops of vanilla ice cream with chocolate syrup. Thank you."

"Well, I . . ."

The smile on Hazel's face was warmer than melted caramel.

The gentleman to Hazel's left held his spoon in the air but it didn't reach his mouth and the ice cream dripped. Hazel smiled.

"Darlin', you're gonna have that all over your shirt in a minute."

It looked as if his eyes would explode. He didn't say anything, just gobbled up the remaining ice cream in his dish, grabbed his hat, and left. In the time it took to say, "What the . . ." Dorothy had placed her bottom on the newly vacant seat.

"Hmmm," she murmured to Hazel, smiling. "It's still warm."

For the next half hour, as white patrons left, some because they'd finished their ice cream and paid, and some because they couldn't countenance sitting next to Black people, the atmosphere of the soda fountain changed from jovial to tense. There was an atmosphere of uneasy anticipation. Something was about to happen, but whether it was good, bad, or indifferent remained to be seen. The waitresses didn't know whether to take orders from the Black WACs or not, the soda jockeys didn't know if they were to fill them, and the manager, a weasel-faced man in his forties, wasn't sure *what* to do. It was the middle of the week and his restaurant was full to bursting with eager, thirsty customers, many of them Negroes. If he didn't serve them, well, he wasn't sure what might happen. There'd been trouble in some parts of the country, and the man didn't want trouble, from Negroes angry at not being served or from white people angry that Negroes were served or from his district supervisor.

His stomach felt like jelly. But as he scanned the restaurant, he calculated the tab for every seat that had a bottom in it, and the total for this one evening exceeded the normal proceeds for three days! The manager was very good at math.

"Serve them," he instructed the staff. "And be quick about it." The weasel-faced man was no fool. If this kept up, his soda fountain would be one of the highest grossing in the region. He was already calculating his pay raise.

Mud, Mud, and More Mud

Fall 1943
Ft. Riley, Kansas

Years later when the captain recalled "her war," she would chuckle and remark that she had never heard a silence so loud as when the unit of Negro WACs posted to Ft. Riley entered their quarters for the first time. She was a sergeant then. Except for the intermittent whine of the wind rattling the window panes—and there was always some bit of wind whooshing across the Kansas plains whatever the season—there was no sound. Not a word, gasp, or sigh from any of the women, hardly the whisper of a breath taken. At least, not at first. Once a minute or two passed, the captain remembered a chorus of exclamations and colorful remarks.

"Well, I guess we'll have to make something work out of

nothing," this from Hazel, the queen of understatements, as she scanned the cavernous frontier-barracks-like room. An expression of dismay had formed on her face.

Edna was never at a loss for words.

"Only thing you can make from shit is a turd," she barked.

"Amen," Dorothy murmured.

As they studied their new surroundings, the women couldn't help but appreciate the irony of their situation. Even considering the plain housing at Ft. Devens and the cramped but comfortable (and warm) accommodations in the hotels of downtown Des Moines, the grim-looking wooden structures were not what they expected, no doubt about it. But when the trucks dropped them off at the gates and they marched in formation through the grounds, past the massive hospital complex then into the barracks areas, they'd had reason to be optimistic. The spartan housing, some of it left over from the late nineteenth century, was well-constructed of brick and wood and in good repair. They'd been told that their quarters were equipped with heat and hot water and, after the long uncomfortable train ride from Des Moines to Kansas, nearly every woman was looking forward to a shower, if not a bath.

But they marched past the officers' housing, the nurses' and NCOs' barracks, and past a plain but substantial building they were told would be occupied by German POWs. They marched past the laundry and the laboratory and some of the athletic fields. And they continued to march until the paved roads merged with gravel roads and the gravel roads merged with dirt roads and the dirt roads merged with mud.

"Attention!" the sergeant called. "Ladies, your quarters. Fall out!"

The barracks rested on stilts, sturdy wooden posts planted in the thick concrete-like Kansas mud. They looked more like rustic camp cottages than military quarters. "With rustic being the operative word," Dorothy commented, wondering not for the last time just what she had gotten herself into. Inside, the ancient buildings were cold, rough-looking, and dirty. And when one of the women asked about heat—it was late September but chilly as if Kansas was preparing herself for a brutal winter—the sergeant shrugged and pointed to the perimeters of the hall where ancient potbellied stoves held court next to ridiculously small coal bins.

"There's more coal outside in the sheds," she said.

"About that shower you were thinking of, Branch?" Edna quipped.

"You've got to be kidding," Rainey growled as she looked around. "I thought I'd left potbellied stoves behind in North Carolina."

"I need a cigarette," Dorothy said, nudging Edna, who always had a good supply.

Edna chuckled.

"Doro, you don't smoke."

Dorothy sighed.

"I might have to start."

*   *   *

It was a rough beginning because, like every other posting they'd been given, there'd been no serious thought to what to do with the women, white or Black. It was as if the army's "prior planning prevents piss-poor performance" motto was thrown out the window like the contents of an overflowing chamber pot. For the first few weeks, they lived out of their duffel bags, uncertain of what was next. There was no direction from the CO as to orders or housing assignments. ("I think this may be it," Dorothy observed unhappily.) For the nurses, essential to the old Ft. Riley cavalry post now that it was a military hospital, the solution came quickly. Housing was readied and duty assignments made. But once the secretarial positions for the CO and other ranking officers were filled, along with a small contingent of WACs assigned to the USO and service clubs, there were literally dozens of women left over. Not so much because there weren't positions to be filled but because there was a lack of common sense. The officer in charge, a major, thought it was ridiculous that women should be in the army in the first place even as he saw increasing numbers of men shipped off to Europe and knew that their positions at the fort would have to be filled. It was inevitable. Ft. Riley had to continue operations. But as far as Negro women were concerned, he didn't see a place for them at all.

"Send 'em to the lab!" he bellowed finally, chuckling. It seemed to him such a clever idea that he was amazed he hadn't thought of it sooner.

The laboratory staff conducted medical and other experiments and testing on a variety of animals but especially on rats and rabbits, which were kept in cages. Located in a remote, undeveloped ("Which means muddy!" exclaimed Leila) area of the hospital complex, a small contingent of WACs that included Leila, Hazel, and Dorothy were assigned to "lab duty."

"Which means clean out the shit," Hazel grumbled.

"And get bitten for your trouble," Dorothy added, crouching low to get a good look at the animals crowded into cages. They looked scared, hungry, and dangerous.

It took no time at all for the revolt to take place.

The major expected to hear crying and screams from the women in the rear lab area and looked forward to the prospect. Because he planned to tell those nigra women that this was their assignment, he was the officer in charge, and if they didn't like it, they could get the hell out of his army. He did not expect to see his office fill up with a dozen or more angry colored women telling him in a chorus of fury that they would not accept this assignment, officer in charge or not. There was not a tear in sight.

One of the women, who acted as the spokesman, a tall lean girl with catlike golden eyes, black hair, and cheekbones sharp enough to cut, glared at him. She looked like a witch. The major didn't know what to think.

"Beg your pardon, Major," she barked, her accent blunt as a club.

He cut her off right there. It was time to get control of this situation.

"You can beg my pardon all you want, Private," he yelled, glad that his muscular Brooklyn-bred bellow covered her strong contralto. "You gals get right back in there; herd up those goddamn rabbits, rats, and what have yous; and clean out those cages! Do you hear me, Private?"

Queens-born Barbara lowered her head like a tiger preparing to pounce and locked eyes with the major. Behind her the murmurs of her sister WACs quieted to a low hum.

"With all due respect, sir," she said, using a tone that resonated with no respect at all, "we're not doing that."

* * *

"'Goddamn nigger WACs.'"

"He said that? To your face?"

Barbara from Queens grinned and nodded.

"The exact quote is 'What the hell is wrong with those goddamn nigger WACs?'"

Dorothy shrugged.

"We've been called worse."

"You got a response at least," Leila commented.

Barbara nodded enthusiastically.

"Orders and assignments are in the works, girls, once the assessments are completed," she said. "And while it won't be a spring walk in the park"—she paused—"this being Kansas and all, at least it won't involve lab rats."

After the revolt, a few quiet "words" were exchanged between the base commander and the major. Shortly after that, the women were evaluated and assigned. The CO, who'd reviewed the files, was incredulous as well as apoplectic. He gestured toward a stack of tan file folders and nearly swept them from his desk.

"Where the hell did all these educated nigras come from?"

The women were delighted—even if many of the assignments were less than glamorous. "This is the army, after all," Edna reminded them. The officers in charge were delighted too, once they recovered from their astonishment. They had the benefit of a literate and well-educated workforce. Leila's aptitude test results, job history, and typing speed qualified her for the medical records secretarial pool. Edna and Rainey, who'd worked in retail as well as in hotel administration, were sent to Special Services, where they managed the Red Cross and USO service club and guesthouses. The major, still angry from his encounter with Barbara from Queens, was almost speechless after he reviewed Hazel's file, whose aptitude test results and job history forms highlighted her education at Oberlin College. He sent for her.

"Ah . . . Private . . . er . . . Diggs . . ."

"Sir." Hazel kept her expression neutral to mask the amusement she felt.

"You studied the piano? At the Oberlin Conservatory?" The major could not hide the surprise in his voice. He thought of himself as a naturally gifted singer in the tenor range, who could have graced the stage at La Scala had he had the opportunity.

"What kind of piano do you play?" he asked. "I mean what kind of music."

Hazel cleared the laughter from her throat.

"I can play it all," Hazel answered calmly. "Everything from hymns to blues to Chopin."

"You're assigned to the hospital library, is that right?" the major asked as an idea formed in his mind. "You and Private Thom?" Dorothy's library experience made her perfect for that assignment. "But perhaps you could play the piano for church services on Sunday? If you had the time . . ." he added, scheming as he spoke. "Accompany the choir and such and, perhaps, a few soloists. We have occasional musical evenings."

Hazel raised one arched eyebrow but suppressed a smile. She'd have this major eating out of her hand in no time.

"I'd be happy to, sir."

The closet operatic tenor's heart skipped a beat. Finally! There was someone on this godforsaken backwater post who could properly accompany him! His mind filled with an image of himself onstage, formally dressed, singing "Nessun dorma." Or "La donna è mobile."

Thou Shalt Not Volunteer

Our girls did every job.

—AZALIA IRENE WILLIAMS OLIVER

'm dead."

Comments of derision, snorts, and hoots of laughter followed this remark from Rainey Barbour. The women were taking advantage of the no-woman's-land, so called because it was the only time of day when they weren't either at work, falling in or out, marching in formation, or otherwise engaged in army-mandated activities. It was a sliver of time between sweat and sleep. Dinner was over but lights out was still to come and the women passed the time by gossiping, playing cards, tidying up their personal spaces, or resting.

"It's your own fault," snapped Edna. "Of all the army rules to break, you broke the golden one."

"Uh, which one is that?" asked Leila, half in and half out of the conversation because she had just finished reading a letter from her mother and was gazing, with tears in her eyes, at a snapshot of her son. Paris seemed to have grown a foot since she'd last seen him.

"Thou shalt not volunteer for any damn thing," Edna said, exhaling a cloud of smoke from her Lucky Strike.

Rainey rolled her eyes, stretched her arms over her head, and groaned.

"Yeah, yeah, well, it's a good thing I did," she said in her slow North Carolina drawl. "If I hadn't, you'd either be starvin' to death or . . . well, starvin' to death."

"Amen to that," Leila commented, catching up to the conversation. "Whatever they served us the first day? It looked like . . . well. Let's just say I've never seen mashed potatoes that looked like that."

"Low-Rainey, you a saint and that's for sure!" Dorothy added, smiling.

It was four months after the dustup with Major Rizzoli over the lab rats. The women had job assignments all over the Ft. Riley post. They managed to embed themselves in the fabric of the old cavalry post and were now practically indispensable, from the USO clubs to the admin secretarial pool to the kitchen. Dorothy and Hazel reorganized the administration of the hospital library, much to the horror of the "Gray Ladies," the hospital's now unneeded librarian volunteers. And when she wasn't researching Dewey decimal cards, Hazel played the piano for church on Sundays, rehearsing the choir every Wednesday at six and reserving an hour weekly to accompany Major Rizzoli, who was preparing Figaro's aria from

The Barber of Seville for a recital he was giving at the end of the month. Hazel was, he boasted to his fellow officers, his personal accompanist.

"Wait. I'm not an opera expert, but . . ." A furrow appeared between Dorothy's eyebrows. "Isn't Figaro a baritone? I thought the major was a tenor."

This brought a bark of laughter from Hazel.

"He is," she confirmed then added, sarcastically, "but he has convinced himself that he has a broad range and can manage the lower register equally well."

Dorothy rolled her eyes.

"I see."

Hazel rolled her eyes as well.

"Lucky you only get to see. I get to actually *hear*."

And after an evening meal at Ft. Riley several weeks after her arrival, Rainey stood up and marched away from the table to the kitchen behind the mess hall where she announced to a group of startled cooks and KP workers that the slop they'd served was so bad that the lab animals wouldn't eat it and that she was there to teach those sad sacks how to cook. Her fried chicken, gravy, green beans, and mashed potato dinner—served the next day—was a testament to her talents and exempted her from any time in the brig for insubordination. She was reassigned and promoted to spec sergeant in charge of KP.

"Who's next?"

All eyes turned to the doorway, where Minn Murphy stood wrapped in a bath towel.

A harmony of groans was her answer as several women stood, stretched, then grabbed their coats. The antiquated water-heating system was coal powered, and the women took turns banking the fires so that each group would have hot water for showers. Doro, Leila, and Hazel pulled on their boots and trudged outside, grumbling as they went but looking forward to the warm water that would be their reward. But there was no reward or consolation for the fact that a group of German POWs, recently arrived on post, were housed in one of the renovated brick buildings that had been modernized with steam heat and modern indoor plumbing.

The inequities stung. The women assigned to the laundries managed the harsh process as well as they could standing in several inches of water every day, winter and summer. Without the "arctics," sturdy lace-up boots allotted to each woman specifically designed for cold weather, the laundry workers would have no protection on their feet at all. These WACs suffered more than their share of health challenges from standing in the moist environment on a wet concrete floor. The women were reassigned once the POWs arrived. The German men took over the laundry operations but not before demanding and receiving wooden platforms at their workstations so that *they* wouldn't have to endure the cold standing water as the women had.

"Aren't *they* the enemy?" one of the women exclaimed in frustration to whomever was within earshot.

"They're white," Hazel responded from behind the book that she was reading. "And we're . . . not."

"We should have been born in Germany," Dorothy commented one day as she, Leila, and Hazel walked past the athletic field on their way to the bus stop. Yelling and whoops of laughter caught their attention as they passed by. Guarded by MPs, the POWs jumped, ran, and kicked their soccer ball so it whooshed across the field. Dorothy wasn't familiar with the game but enjoyed watching the men play and thought it might be fun to try it someday. The sound of a sharp kick was followed by the actual ball bouncing in front of them on its way across the road. Dorothy skipped behind it and finally caught it. As she turned toward the field, she heard voices raised and one in particular coming from a man gesturing at her to throw the ball, his mouth wide with a smile. He called out again. But as Dorothy positioned herself to return the ball, she paused.

"What is it?" Leila asked, noticing that Doro's expression had changed from a pleasant smile to a face of stone. "What's wrong?" She and Hazel exchanged glances. In the time they'd known Dorothy, rarely did she look angry or upset. Now she looked furious.

Dorothy adjusted the ball between her palms, raised it, and threw it forcefully—in the opposite direction of the soccer field. What followed was the sound of men's voices, angry and shouting. Then she picked up the backpack that she'd set down and marched on toward the bus stop for the short ride to town with the other women sprinting to catch up with her.

"Doro, what the . . . what did he say?" Leila asked. "I didn't get any of his words. I don't speak German. Do you?"

Dorothy's face remained marble-like.

"Enough to understand *him*," she said coldly. "He said, 'Throw the ball, nigger.'"

Then Dorothy grinned.

"So I did."

FEMALE PROBLEMS

For years afterwards, Dorothy could think of only one word to describe her army experience: "waiting." Waiting to fall in or fall out. Waiting in queue at the mess, standing at attention, waiting. Waiting for inspection. And then, there was "furlough," a dressed up word for "waiting." Now, Dorothy was waiting again. But this interlude to mark the passage of time was more excruciating than previous ones.

The army had finally found a job for them, for the Negro WACs. No one knew what that job was or where it was. Even the Ft. Riley top brass professed to know nothing. And the soon-to-be-designated commanding officer, Major Charity Adams, who was still posted at Ft. Des Moines, knew only that a job had been found. But the call went out for volunteers and, despite the admonition of "Never volunteer!" many women applied. Interviews were set up, psychological and aptitude test administered, physical exams endured. One intriguing tidbit leaked out: those chosen would first report to the Overseas Training Center at Ft. Oglethorpe, Georgia, for combat training.

Dorothy submitted an application, and now there was nothing to do but wait until the decisions were made. She tried to keep her mind on her work but she couldn't. The possibility of serving overseas, even though nothing had been said about *that*, was her dream come true. It was so exciting to contemplate that she couldn't sleep or concentrate. The library became a looking glass world. Dorothy placed books on the cart the wrong way in, misfiled the Dewey decimal cards, and organized the "Books on Hold" shelf so badly that she gave a sergeant major the two gothic romances set aside for one of the nurses instead of the Zane Grey westerns that he had reserved.

"Thom! What is the matter with you?" Hazel asked. "You've shelved the *P*s with the *D*s and . . . I don't even see the *C*s!"

"Sorry," Dorothy murmured, quickly gathering up the books to reshelve them. "Has the mail pouch come today?"

"You're either in a fog or you got ants in your pants," Hazel continued her tirade as she helped her friend. "Honestly, you'd better shake yourself out of the . . . Oh!" She glanced at Dorothy as the realization entered her mind. She lowered her voice. "You haven't heard anything yet?"

Dorothy shook her head slowly.

"Not a word. But then no one's heard anything."

Hazel shrugged.

"It's the army way," she said, turning her attention back to the book cart. "Hurry up and wait. Then wait some more."

Dorothy sighed.

And make myself crazy thinking about it. Combat training!

Dorothy could barely contain herself. She'd heard bits and pieces of what it entailed, and it sounded thrilling! Gas masks, rope climbing, obstacle courses! She tried to entice her friends to apply but only Leila accepted the challenge. Hazel was not enthused and decided to pass on the opportunity, especially after she was offered a Special Services post at Camp Knight in Oakland where her current beau was stationed.

"Excuse me." A young PFC—Hardin was her name—approached the counter.

"Thom, have you seen Branch? She isn't at her desk in the clinic." The PFC looked over her shoulder then added in a whisper, "She's a half hour late getting back from her break."

Dorothy frowned. *That's not like Leila*, she thought.

"I wouldn't bother you," the WAC continued, "except I know that you and Branch are close. I thought that you might know where she is."

They looked everywhere. And the longer they looked, the more concerned Dorothy became. The hospital was a massive complex consisting of labyrinthine mazes of corridors and hallways, designed by what had to be a disturbed individual who relished the thought of medical staff and personnel becoming disoriented and lost. Dorothy and Hardin stopped in the courtyard and spoke with a retired warrant officer whom Leila had befriended. She read the newspapers to him once a week because his eyesight was failing. He hadn't seen her. They checked the gymnasium and the water therapy rooms where Leila occasionally helped out. No luck. They walked through the cafeteria and even checked the PX, although Leila wasn't much of a shopper with the exception of chocolates. Finally, after a half hour of frustration, Dorothy had the bright idea to stop in the ladies' room just outside the clinic secretarial pool where Leila worked. And this is where she found her friend, groaning and holding her abdomen, her face twisted with pain and drained of color.

Somehow, Dorothy and Private Hardin commandeered a wheelchair and got her to the women's ward of the primary hospital.

"Over here." Nurse Sally Francis gestured toward an empty bed. Glancing around the ward, Dorothy noticed that they were surrounded by a sea of white blankets and white faces. "Shouldn't we take her to the Negro ward?" she whispered to Sally, the only Negro RN on duty.

The nurse grinned. "We only have one Negro patient." She nodded toward Leila. "So, by extension, this *is* the Negro ward." She patted Leila gently on the arm. "Wait here. I'll get a doctor."

Dorothy nodded.

"Hardin," she spoke to the private. "If you don't mind . . ."

"I'll tell Miss Hazel where you are," Hardin answered. "Don't worry."

Returning to the library to finish her shift wasn't what Dorothy was worried about. She tried to comfort Leila, who writhed from side to side on the bed, clutching her belly with clenched fists. Leila's monthlies were a crapshoot, as Aunt Denie would have said. Some months they passed without giving her more than a twitch. Other months she was wracked with pain and experienced heavy bleeding. And still other months, Leila managed to maneuver through a devil's cocktail of annoying cramps paired with intermittent bleeding. But this was one of the bad ones.

The sound of footsteps distracted Dorothy from her reverie. Looking up, she saw Sally approaching and behind her, Dr. Brimwell. Dorothy felt her stomach drop. Now she had something else to worry about.

"Only doc on duty," Sally whispered as she passed Dorothy.

Captain Alistair Brimwell was young, a Harvard med graduate, a gynecological specialist, and a hater of women and Negroes. The consensus among the WACs, Negro and white, was that he'd had a complicated relationship with his mother and was taking it out on women in general.

"He should choose another specialty," a white lieutenant said. "The sadist."

An admittedly Freudian-inspired observation, but what other explanation could there be? The Negro WACs swore that he was a card-carrying member of the Klan. He wore his disdain on his sleeve and spoke in a smooth voice dripping with condescension.

"Everything but the sheets," Hazel had commented after enduring a routine exam administered by the doctor.

Disturbing stories moved quickly along the WAC's grapevines like undercurrents, their substance invisible on the placid surface but brutal and deadly below. It started with the WACs assigned to work in the laundry, one of the most rigorous and grueling posts. The hours were long, the work physically taxing, and the conditions grim if not primitive. The laundry was either too hot or too cold, and the women spent the entire shift standing in several inches of water on a rock-hard concrete floor. It was a toxic cock-tail, and within three months, illness set up a comfortable home in the soupy, humid mildew-scented building. Colds, stomach ailments, headaches, and swollen feet paired with leg cramps brought many of the women low.

"Those gals are always sick," Hazel observed.

Dorothy felt a chill across her shoulders.

It seemed to Dorothy, and she wasn't alone in thinking this way, that too many of the women who went to the hospital for "women's troubles" ended up in surgery. "To see what's going on in there," the doctors said. You signed your name, inhaled some gas, and went to sleep. Post-op was a blur; the diagnosis was a mystery. Eventually, there was recovery and then relief that the pain was gone. Only later, amidst murmurs and whispers, were pointed questions asked and eventually answered, and the women learned that their wombs were also gone. It happened too often to be a coincidence.

"You can leave now, girl," Brimwell barked. "On your way."

Dorothy bristled.

"If you don't mind, sir, Private Branch and I are like sisters. I don't want to leave her alone. I know she'll feel better with me here." Dorothy affected Aunt Denie's voice and manner, the one she used for white folks whom she neither liked nor trusted.

Just put enough sugah in it to keep you from bein' lynched.

Surprisingly, Brimwell acquiesced. Sally raised an eyebrow.

"Suit yourself. Now I have questions, Private."

Methodically, the doctor reviewed Leila's medical history,

pausing only after she mentioned that she had had a child. More than that, Leila did not say. Motherhood and the military did not go together.

"Hmmm," Brimwell commented. "And you are unmarried." It was a verdict.

And it will damn her, Dorothy thought.

"Yes, sir," Leila managed, her usually clear voice dull and hoarse because of the pain.

The doctor jotted a few lines on the chart, then spoke over his shoulder to Sally.

"We'll get you comfortable," Brimwell cooed. "Tomorrow, we'll take you into surgery." He patted Leila's arm—she flinched—and he smiled. "And we'll find out what's going on in there."

"Nurse Francis, the pain meds," Brimwell said in a sharp tone as he swept away.

Sally waited a few moments until the doctor was out of earshot, then whispered to Dorothy, "I'll get her settled. But we've got to find a way to keep her out of surgery. Because once she's under, whether she needs it or not, he'll take everything out."

DEAD OR ALIVE

They had less than twenty-four hours.

Leila needed help. The question was, what kind of help? Considering Brimwell's reputation, the only "help" Leila would get was a hysterectomy. Sally wasn't sure that such drastic surgical intervention was necessary, but her opinion didn't count: she was a nurse not a doctor. What Leila needed was a second opinion.

Dorothy and Hazel dissected the problem as they walked back to the library.

"Doro. You don't think she could . . . d-die, do you?" Hazel's voice cracked. "She's just a kid!"

Dorothy shook her head and quickly wiped away a tear with the back of her hand. *And we're in the middle of a war. Leila can't die! Not now. There's so much death already.*

"Course not," she snapped in a voice draped with more certainty than she felt. "There must be something that we . . ."

Suddenly, Dorothy stopped.

"What about that doctor that Geneva's always going on about?"

Hazel's brows furrowed as she tried to remember.

"What doctor?"

"You know," Dorothy prodded. "The one she calls '*her* doctor'; she calls him every time she has a hangnail. He served with her father somewhere in . . ." Dorothy snapped her fingers. "World War I! Her father was posted in France, with the 369th! She talks about them all the time."

Hazel increased her pace. "Let's go find out!"

Dorothy checked her watch. "Knowing Geneva, she's either in the barracks because she made a sick call today or she's at work in . . ."

Hazel chuckled.

"Geneva? At work?"

Geneva Brown was the only daughter in a family of boys and was not above using any advantage she could think of to gain a lighter work duty and other benefits.

"I'll bet you a pack of Parliaments that she's in the barracks, nursing a paper cut," Hazel murmured as she and Dorothy sprinted toward their lodgings.

"Not taking that bet, thank you," Dorothy countered. "Don't have the wherewithal to lose this week!"

Hazel was right.

"What?" Geneva yelped when Dorothy grabbed her foot and swung it across the bed. "I've got a tummy thing today! Can't you see I'm sick?"

Dorothy and Hazel exchanged glances.

Geneva was the poster child of blooming health.

"Neva, what's the name of that doctor you talk about? The one who served with your dad in France?"

Geneva pouted.

"You mean Captain Lazlo? My doctor?"

Dorothy permitted herself an eye roll.

"Yes, Neva, *your* doctor. His name is Lazlo? Where is he assigned?"

"Why?" Geneva asked, not even pretending to be helpful. "There are other . . ."

"Neva! Leila's in trouble, okay? She's having a bad period this month, so bad that she's in ward five and Brimwell's pushing for surgery."

Geneva's eyes widened.

"Oh. He works out of the seventh ward on the third floor. Just tell him I told you . . ."

"Thanks, Neva!" Dorothy yelled over her shoulder as she ran out of the barracks with Hazel at her heels.

Dorothy and Hazel had not walked but run through the ward. Dr. Alan Lazlo listened to the women's story without interrupting as it was recounted quickly between gasps while they caught their breath. He knew immediately what to do even though he also knew that it was unwise and risky. Brimwell outranked him. Brimwell was also a nasty piece of work. The comments he'd overheard . . .

I'd rather see rats procreate than kikes or niggers.

"I'll look in on Private Branch," he said. "But there is one caveat—if I conclude that her condition indicates that a hysterectomy is advised, then I'll tell her. And I'll tell her straight. But if not . . ." His words trailed off.

Dorothy's shoulders tightened. She was afraid for Leila.

"If not?" Dorothy asked. She and the doctor locked eyes.

Lazlo didn't have to think about his answer.

"I'll handle it," he said.

It was two o'clock in the morning. The ward was quiet except for the intermittent snoring of one of the patients, and the lights were low. The nurse on duty had stepped away from her station to heat water for a cup of tea. And for this time of year, the often volatile atmosphere of the plains was unseasonably calm; no delinquent winds paid a nocturnal visit. It would have been easy for Leila to dismiss what happened next as a dream. But as it happened, the pain pills had worn off and she was wide awake, uncomfortably so, and squirming to find a comfortable position in the unfamiliar hospital bed. When she noticed a tall shadowy figure approaching, she tensed with fear. Leila hadn't closely followed the conversation between Doro, Hazel, Nurse Sally, and the doctor. She'd been in and out of any awareness due to the pain. But the stories about some of the doctors here were widely shared. And this doctor in particular, the one who'd examined her, had an ominous reputation. Leila's hands formed into fists.

The specter leaned down. Leila felt his breath in her ear.

"Private Branch."

The man had dark hair and a long slender face with barely any cheekbones, and he wore black glasses. He was not Dr. Brimwell. But . . .

"I'm Dr. Lazlo, Captain Lazlo. Your friends, Privates Thom and

Diggs, asked me to look in on you." He pulled something out of his pocket. The doctor's voice was low and deep, two steps above a whisper but just loud enough for Leila to hear. "May I?"

Leila felt the coolness of his hand as he took her pulse and gently touched her forehead like her mother used to do.

"How are you feeling? Are you in any pain?"

He moved like a wraith, silently but with purpose, sliding the medical chart out of its tray. He used a cigarette lighter to read the notes.

"Private? Are you having any pain?" he asked again.

Leila whispered, "Yes."

The doctor nodded.

"I'll get you something. How is the bleeding?"

Leila swallowed.

"It's still . . . just a little."

"All right. I see from your chart that you have difficult menstruation from time to time." He clicked off the lighter. "This is one of those times?"

"Yes," Leila said.

"Cramps?"

She nodded.

"You have a child, is that correct?"

Was he trying to trick her?

Leila felt her defenses rising. Whenever that question was asked, she always felt as if the judgment of God would come down on her shoulders, that, as a scarlet woman, she would be cast out. She took a breath.

"Yes. Paris. He's almost three."

The doctor nodded.

"I remember when my daughter was that age," he commented. "Was your pregnancy normal? Any problems during the delivery?"

The doctor's only reaction to Leila's answers were "Good" and "All right."

He said nothing for a moment, then explained that he was going to do an examination, and specified how and where he would touch her and what he hoped to learn by doing so. Leila closed her eyes and took a deep breath. It would be okay, wouldn't it? Doro and Hazel wouldn't have sent someone who would hurt her. Right?

"I want you to listen carefully, Private. I'm going to tell you what my diagnosis is and what I think we should do. You have some choices here, but they are yours alone. My job is to tell you what they are. Do you understand?"

Tears rolled down Leila's face and she nodded.

"No, Private. I need to hear you say it."

"Yes. I understand."

*   *   *

According to her medical chart, Private Leila Branch's condition took a turn for the worse overnight, which created the need for an immediate evaluation by the physician on call. After his consultation with the patient and a physical exam, a minor surgical intervention took place, and by the time Captain Alistair Brimwell stepped into the ward at 0900, Private Branch was resting comfortably. Nurse Sally noted later that Brimwell didn't appear to be either disappointed or suspicious. He scanned the chart, noting that a minor procedure had taken place and that the patient had responded well. If he was surprised that Lazlo was on duty that night, considering that he'd been the second on a long, complicated surgery the day before, he didn't comment. Brimwell barely gave the sleeping patient a glance.

Dr. Lazlo ordered bed rest and light duty for his patient, only releasing her to the barracks after he was satisfied that she was no longer in pain. Leila recovered quickly and from the day of her release, Alan Lazlo became "her doctor" too, although she hoped that she would never again spend time in a Ft. Riley hospital ward. Her wish was not granted.

Logistics, shortages, and miscommunication left a hole in the nursing staff roster that would not be filled for weeks. The primary nursing corps was transferred en masse without replacements and the brass scrambled. Every remaining WAC on post was immediately assigned to the hospital until the replacement unit of nurses transferred in. The head nurse wanted to take to her bed. In a matter of days, she had to transform laundry workers, hospitality club managers, secretaries, and librarians into duty nurses.

Not everyone was up to the task.

Dorothy flinched as she handled the hypodermic needle with trembling fingers. She'd never given an injection in her life.

"Just don't stick it in an artery," the nurse instructor said lightheartedly. "That would be messy."

Geneva took sick call after two days of training.

Hazel fainted at the sight of blood.

"You want me to touch that?" a WAC named Ruby barked. "If I'm gonna put my hands there . . . then I'll need a cigarette. Or three," she added, cool as a cucumber as if commenting on the weather. The only reason Ruby wasn't reprimanded was because the hospital needed staff. Desperately. She lit her cigarette.

After a week on the wards, Dorothy was smoking too. After three weeks—with nary a unit of replacement nurses in sight—there was a revolt. Another one.

If the Black women didn't want to be working as nurses in the hospital, then it was also true that the patients and some of the doctors didn't want them working there either.

"Hey, nigger! Here's a bedpan for ya!"

"Wash your hands good. I don't want that black rubbing off on me."

"You colored gals sure are mean. I want to hear you singing as you work! Aren't you Negroes happy?"

"I'd rather die than let some nigger bitch give me a shot."

"That can be arranged," Dorothy growled as she imagined herself lunging toward the wheelchair-bound soldier who'd made the remark.

Tempers were high. At the point that it took three women to restrain Dorothy—who was one of the most even-tempered women on the ward—the officer in charge, a Captain Froh, decided that enough was enough. And for the fourth time in as many weeks, she ordered the women to dress, fall in, and march in formation to the CO's office—this time at seven in the morning. The colonel hadn't had his second cup of coffee and had just finished shaving in the small lavatory within his office.

"What the . . . Captain?" The colonel frowned. Captain Elizabeth Froh was usually the picture of serenity; her features and calm demeanor reminded him, for some reason, of that painting, the one of the woman with her hands folded in her lap. "*Mona Lisa*. That's it," he thought. "The *Mona Lisa*." The colonel noted that Captain Froh did not look calm or serene now.

"Colonel, sir." Captain Froh saluted and waited.

"At ease, Captain," the colonel said. "What seems to be the problem?" He noted the band of women standing in formation behind her. Soon, he would wish that he hadn't asked.

"My substitute nurses, sir," the captain stated without preamble. "Filling in until the replacements arrive? They are ready to mutiny. They have said that they won't go back to the wards until something is done. They have put up with insults, ugly language, inappropriate touching, and other . . . conduct unbecoming, sir."

Mutiny? The colonel's only experience with mutiny was in literature. *But "conduct unbecoming"?*

"I see."

"This is the fourth time, sir," Captain Froh continued.

The colonel said nothing. He could count. The captain and the colored WACs had been on his doorstep three times over the past month, each time to deliver a litany of misbehavior by the soldier patients on the wards.

"The women are fed up, Colonel. Either the behavior stops or . . . well, when are the replacement nurses expected to arrive?"

The one question that the colonel hoped she would not ask because he had just been advised of another delay.

"No ETA set, Captain," the colonel answered unhappily.

The captain's lips pressed together and formed a straight line of disapproval.

"I am concerned, sir. The morale of my women is very low. It's not the blood, smells, or . . . unpleasant sights that have brought them down, sir. It's the behavior of the men with their rough manners." The captain paused to allow the impact of her comments and the concerns embedded within them, unsaid, to sink in.

The colonel got the message loud and clear. He had a daughter. But *these* women . . .

"I will address the situation, Captain," he said, his voice grim.

The memo was distributed the next day. Any soldier who was a patient in the medical center was to behave himself, not use abusive language or insults or a tone that he would not use with his family members. Every patient was to keep his hands to himself. And should any inappropriate behavior or speech be observed, it was to be reported and said soldier would be written up and discharged from the hospital immediately, regardless of medical condition or situation, whether he was dead or alive.

The colonel signed the order with great displeasure. He hated being placed in this situation, but he needed these women to stay on duty until replacements arrived. As he dotted the *i* in his name, he murmured to himself, "Goddamn nigger WACs."

The Battalion

They found a job for us.
—DOROTHY TURNER JOHNSON

Winter 1944–45
Ft. Oglethorpe, Georgia

n the fall of 1944, the tides of the war shifted. Then in December, they shifted again with deadly effects. Winter set in on the continent, bringing cold, snow, and on the sixteenth of December, the campaign that came to be called "the Battle of the Bulge." Dorothy's grasp of military strategy and actions was rudimentary at best, but word of what was happening spread quickly. Everyone, whether in uniform or not, held their breath. Plans were made and unmade, initiatives plotted, then taken apart and reworked. The Germans were numerous and seemed unstoppable. Eisenhower expedited reinforcements. And the Third Army under Lt. Colonel Patton pivoted north to push the Germans back. Would it work?

Almost from the day in 1941 that the United States joined the war, American families sent their sons to fight. To keep their ties strong with home, American mothers and fathers also sent letters, care packages, birthday gifts, and treasures to reinforce the love and pride they felt. But as the troops moved quickly from place to place to support the battles and hostilities, it became obvious that letters from home could not follow their intended recipients. As the war dragged on, the mail piled up, stored in unused airplane hangars and warehouses in Birmingham, Rouen, and Paris, despite the devastation wrought by German bombers. Every few days, US military trucks, behemoths that spewed diesel fuel and groaned like giant beetles, rolled up to these designated buildings and dumped the precious words penned on perfumed stationery (sealed with lipstick kisses) along with packages containing cakes, cookies, wristwatches, and clothing from anxious parents, wives, and girlfriends who wanted to ensure that their "boys" knew that they weren't forgotten, that they would be fed enough (diets supplemented with cakes and cookies) and be warm enough (hand-knitted sweaters and scarves) in the bleak, damp continental winters. It was to have been a temporary solution. By January 1945, when the Allies had the Germans within their sights, the stockpiles of undelivered mail had grown into mountains of paper, extending within feet of the cavernous airplane hangars' ceilings.

Major Charity Adams was on a plane flying over the Atlantic toward Bermuda when she opened the first envelope containing her orders, and she was in London when she learned that her mission was to organize and command a postal directory service stationed in Birmingham, England, to oversee the processing and delivery of the stockpiled and undelivered mail. The unit was assigned to a building formerly occupied by St. Edward's, a boys' school, now requisitioned by the US Army. Adams had less than a month to get the facility furnished, supplied, and staffed.

The first group of WACs would arrive by boat at Glasgow in early February, the second group at the end of March. There were to be 855 women in all, Privates Dorothy Thom, Leila Branch, and Hazel Diggs among them.

Before the rolling sensation of the north Atlantic, before boarding the luxurious RMS *Queen Mary*, before the excitement set in, there was yet another furlough. And then there was combat training at Ft. Oglethorpe.

I wanted adventure and I sure got it!

Dorothy sank onto her bunk. Better to say that she sank *into* her bunk. *Correct English be damned*, she said to herself. She was too tired to care. Every bone in her body hurt, every muscle ached. Dorothy had been crawling (and not just *any* kind of crawling) flat on her stomach, using her arms to move her body forward like a lizard. Through the mud, across the rough, cold earth. *Over the river and through the woods* . . . She inhaled deeply and thought —*That hurt*—then exhaled slowly. That hurt too. *What I need is a long soak in the tub. With a generous helping of Epsom salts.* Her imagination took over. She saw Aunt Emmie wearing her calm, professional licensed-practical-nurse expression and her white long-sleeved nurse's uniform, measuring out the salts and pouring them into a claw-foot tub, three-quarters filled. The water was hot, wonderfully hot. The steam rose and morphed into a moist, delicious fog. Dorothy closed her eyes. She could feel the water covering her shoulders, cuddling her like a child in a blanket. *Ummm.* Yes. A bath was in order, then a wrap-up in soft, fluffy towels smelling like fresh summer air, scented by lilacs, warm from drying in the sun on the clothesline in Aunt Denie's backyard . . .

Suddenly, uninvited, reality cut in. The lovely dream faded, replaced by an image of the group showers in the barracks. Cold floor, fogged up windows, flimsy shower curtains, and fluctuating water pressure. Noise, the sounds of water and women's voices echoed from the concrete walls. Not to mention unreliable water temperature. Dorothy sighed. A warm bath was what she needed. A tepid shower was what she'd get.

"A penny for your thoughts, Thom."

Hazel's voice intruded on her reverie but was not unwelcome. Hazel's heart had been set on a California post and a certain sergeant, but the romance faded, and Hazel, who had applied as an afterthought, was accepted to the mysterious overseas assignment. Dorothy opened her eyes and attempted to form a smile.

Hazel whistled.

"You look like what the cat refused to bring in."

Dorothy's chuckle was weak. She was too sore to laugh.

"That's exactly how I feel."

Hazel waved a piece of paper in her direction.

"Well, I have news." Hazel's eyes twinkled. "Orders. We're shipping out. Day after tomorrow. Practically leaving in the middle of the night! Train to New York City, then a transport ship to someplace called Prestwick and then Birmingham." Hazel's smile widened. "Great Britain not Alabama. We're sailing on the SS *Île de France*. How's that for a name?"

Dorothy yawned.

"I heard."

"Did you get orders too?"

Dorothy nodded.

"I certainly did. Furlough."

"What?" Hazel shrieked. "You're not coming over with us?"

"Abou Ben Adhem, may his tribe increase . . ."

Hazel snorted and rolled her eyes.

"That's what I get for making friends with a librarian. Always quoting some dead poet. Tennyson or Dunbar or . . ."

"Leigh Hunt," Dorothy interjected, grinning. "Like Abou, my name is not on the first list. But I'm told we'll get orders to go in a few weeks." She yawned again.

Hazel dug Dorothy's bathing caddy out of her trunk. "Shower, PFC, *now*. You stink. And while you're in there, think about what you're going to do on furlough. Where are you going anyway? To your mother's place in Cleveland?"

"Heaven forbid!" Dorothy said, and she meant it. "No, I'm staying in Georgia. Heading south to Atlanta to see Denie and then out to Eatonton."

Hazel, who was from Kansas City and had never been to Georgia in her life before coming to Ft. Oglethorpe, frowned slightly. "Eatonton?"

"It's . . . the town where my mother was born, just east and south of Atlanta, out in the sticks."

Hazel's expression was pensive.

"Do you still have family there?"

"Yes, some."

Dorothy gathered her shower caddy and towels into her arms.

Hazel was intrigued. "Then why not stay in Atlanta. More bright lights."

Dorothy's mind was far away.

"There's something that I need to do."

*   *   *

The telegram arrived in the summer while she was stationed at Ft. Riley. It had been a busy morning in the hospital library with a sprinkle of glamour that provided a conversation starter to last the rest of the month. With the library situated at the end of a T-shaped corridor, the library staff spent almost as much time managing book circulation traffic as it did people traffic. The hospital was large and could be challenging to maneuver in. On any given day, Dorothy and her colleagues assisted as many library patrons as they did confused personnel looking for this doctor or that ward. They became experts at pointing the men in the right direction or, if the instructions were too confusing, personally escorting a soldier to his destination. This morning, in addition to the usual requests for information, book check-ins and outs, there was an inquiry from a soldier whose injuries were usual but whose face was not.

"Excuse me?"

Dorothy looked up. The soldier wore the standard-issue khaki uniform, but there was nothing standard about the splotches of blood on the front of his shirt, his bruised knuckles, and the bright purple and yellow shiner that encircled his puffy and bloodshot left eye. Mrs. Bieber, the "Gray Lady" volunteer who was manning the circulation desk, gasped.

"Oh my goodness! Is that . . ."

"Yes . . . Private, how may I help you?" Dorothy asked.

"I'm sure I'm lost," the man answered in a pleasant and familiar voice. "The reception clerk directed me left, then right, then . . ." He frowned.

"You want the clinic? Major Nielson?" Dorothy inquired. His colorful, swollen eyelid was a giveaway.

The private nodded with relief.

"Yes. Am I close? I feel as if I've been walking for hours. I think I took a wrong turn somewhere . . ."

Dorothy nodded and came from behind the counter.

"You aren't lost, actually," she said, gesturing toward the end of the corridor. "You just aren't there yet. Continue down this hall, turn right, and take the second door on your left. Dr. Nielson's top-notch. He'll fix you right up." She studied the man's face. "Best to get that eye looked at."

"Thanks so much, ma'am," the private said, his smile expanding in wattage.

Dorothy bit her lip. It must have been quite a fight.

"Um . . . if you don't mind my asking. Who won?"

The round-faced private grinned, then winced.

"I did," he said proudly. Then he lowered his voice. "But I told the guy it was a draw so that he would buy the beers."

Their laughter filled the hallway.

"Well done, soldier," Dorothy said.

"Thank you, ma'am," Private Mickey Rooney said.

Minutes later, Aggie Patterson entered the library. She glanced over her shoulder.

"Was that . . ."

"Yes, it was," Mrs. Bieber said in a smug voice. "Private Thom directed him to the emergency ward."

Aggie's gaze flitted to Dorothy, who winked.

"You never know who you may run into at the Ft. Riley Military Hospital. Dorothy, um, Thom. Captain Ingram sent me to deliver this to you." She held the telegram out. The smile faded from her face. "I hope that it isn't bad news." But of course, as everyone knew, telegrams nearly always were.

It was from her mother in Cleveland.

BIG DAD PASSED YESTERDAY EVENING.

Dorothy didn't have enough leave then to get to Georgia and back. She telegraphed her mother and spent Friday in a state of mind that vacillated between sadness and reflection.

He was a constant presence in her life and the lives of her mother, aunts and uncles, and sisters and brothers for as long as she could remember, stage-managing his family in ways that seemed medieval. He had shrewdly built a platform of stability grounded in education and land ownership that made it possible for his children and grandchildren to follow suit. The white town fathers admired him, patronizing his store and catering business, though they called him "Unc' Jack," a moniker that sent a shudder of distaste through his family.

Dorothy's memories of her grandfather were numerous and contradictory.

"You have to understand what his motivations are," Denie explained to her nieces when they were older. She sounded conciliatory even though she was frequently the target of her father's ire. "He will do anything, did anything, to protect his family from what he had to live through growing up. Dad worked in the fields with his mother from when he could barely walk. He was separated from her after the war—Grandma Mahala got typhoid fever and went into a camp hospital. He saw when she was beaten and when . . ." Denie stopped. Some things did not need to be said.

When Jack was five or six years old, or younger, he watched as one of the men working on the farm was whipped. Mahala, weeping and holding his hand so tightly that he was near weeping himself, whispered to him in a voice full of fury and terror. "Lis'n good, Jack, hear? Lis'n to Momma. Don' never sass nobody and don' never steal. You understand?"

"Yes, Momma."

That was the first lesson Jack learned from his mother's handbook of how to keep himself alive. It would not be the last. The rich Georgia soil nourished grain; cash crops like cotton, corn, cane, and tobacco; and horses, pigs, and cattle. It was ambrosia for flowers. And it fed a certain kind of white man who would kill a Black one as soon as look at him.

He taught himself to read and write and "figure" as he told it. He worked at a hotel, sold ice, made ice cream, and ran errands. And when he asked for Dick the Indian's oldest daughter's hand in marriage, he told Old Man Swanson that he would see to it that his daughter would never work in a white man's house. And she never did.

Cousin Alonzo drove her to the cemetery in his blue Ford truck, of which he was very proud.

"I'll park over there and have a smoke," he said. "You take your time."

"I appreciate that. Thank you, Lonzo," Dorothy answered, stepping down from the truck without hesitation. Thanks to the US Army, she could get in and out of a truck, no problem!

She waved as the truck pulled away, then noticed that she was standing in a puddle. Good thing she remembered to pack her army-issue arctics. January and February in Cleveland and, probably, in Birmingham, England, which was where she was headed, could be very cold and snowy. But January and February in Georgia, while also cold, was almost always wet.

The East Eatonton Cemetery was on low, gritty soil bordering a state road that ran parallel to Gray's Creek. It was the colored cemetery and had been since the war's end in 1865. The ground was uneven and coarse, and Dorothy walked gingerly, her boots making squishy sounds in the moist earth. It was a mild day for February. Dorothy wondered if she should be watchful for snakes. The path rounded toward the road into the oldest section of the cemetery. No poetry or pointed Bible verses adorned these monuments. The information carved was basic, spartan: name, year of birth, year of death.

She saw the two headstones ahead of her, set apart, alone yet together. Each stone was different, one tall and rectangular, the other tall but oval shaped.

JACK MONTGOMERY

1859–1944

HARRIET SWANSON MONTGOMERY

1865–1908

Big Dad had meticulously organized and planned every aspect of his and his children's lives to the best of his power, but he had not planned to outlive his beloved by over thirty years.

She had prepared a personal prayer for this moment but the words were forgotten. Her grandparents had survived enslavement, Reconstruction, night riders, and the dawn of the twentieth century. They had endured and sacrificed and worked—hard—to create the space on which Dorothy now stood. And now, she was preparing to do something that neither of her grandparents could even imagine.

"Thank you," she whispered, wiping the tears from her checks.

*   *   *

Two weeks later, Pfc. Dorothy Thom and Pfc. Leila Branch, along with three hundred African American WACs, set off from the Port of New York aboard the RMS *Queen Mary*, a.k.a. the "Gray Ghost," bound for Glasgow and for their first overseas assignment as part of the US Army's Postal Directory Service for the European theater of operations, officially known as the 6888th Postal Directory Battalion.

Furlough Two

Winter 1944–45
Dayton, Ohio

eila would remember her time on furlough as one question:
"What do you do in the army?"

From Paris, it was "What do you in the army, Mommy?" It was a wonder the little boy was able to get the words out, considering that his mommy was hugging him so tightly. Leila didn't answer her son at first because she was too busy squeezing him, holding and stroking him, sniffing his Dial-soap scented neck and kissing his ripe peach-colored cheeks.

"Mommy! Stop!" the little boy squealed as he batted at his mother, who was planting a raspberry on his soft round tummy.

Leila couldn't get enough of Paris. But Paris was three and a half now and had had quite enough of Leila. When she finally released him, her son placed his palms on her cheeks and held her head still, looking at her with a somber expression. His eyes were unblinking.

"What d'you do in the army, Mommy?"

She told Paris about the marching and the mud at Ft. Riley, the soda fountain drinks across the street from the makeshift hotel barracks that were part of Ft. Des Moines, and the crawling-marching-hiking-climbing at Ft. Oglethorpe. It wasn't surprising that he enjoyed the stories involving mud, crawling, and climbing the most.

"And what's next?" Pearl asked, handing over a shot of whiskey, its amber color amplified by the cut-glass tumbler, used only for company and special occasions.

Leila was surprised at the welcome she received at home. It was as if her mother had been kidnapped and replaced by a woman who now treated her as an adult. Pearl had redecorated Leila's bedroom with new sheets and draperies (that she'd made herself; Pearl was an artist on a Singer sewing machine), leaving lavender-scented sachets in the bureau drawers. The front room—Pearl's pride and joy—had also been redecorated and the new burgundy-colored sofa and matching armchair shared space with a top-of-the-line RCA Victor radio. And, to Leila's amazement, her mother would not let her lift a finger, not to cook, pick up a dirty dish, or even to wash her own lingerie.

"You been through enough," Pearl announced with a nod toward Isaac, who was now more than a fixture in the house. "You just rest and enjoy your boy. He's been worrying me to death about where his mommy is and what she does in the army! Besides . . ."

Leila took a sip of whiskey and smiled as it snaked its way down her throat, warm and smooth.

"Besides?"

Pearl cleared her throat.

"I want you to be fresh and alert when you speak on Sunday afternoon."

Leila choked on the whiskey.

"Speak . . . to . . . speak where? About what?"

Pearl fluffed the pillows on the couch as if they hadn't been fluffed ten minutes ago.

"To the ladies of the Pine Street AME Women's Improvement Club. We meet every third Sunday afternoon, tea and sweets. And we often have a speaker. This Sunday . . ."

"This Sunday!" Leila squeaked. "Mom, what the . . ."

Pearl gave her a dark look.

"Watch your language, Leila Doreen Branch. You may be grown but you're still *my* child."

Leila rolled her eyes.

"Mom."

"This Sunday I said that you would be happy to talk to the ladies about your experience in the WACs. About the women you've met and your training. And about where you're going next. Which is . . ." Pearl waited expectantly.

"Which is a place that I can't mention yet, Mom," Leila said firmly.

"Oh, all right," Pearl conceded, a bit too quickly in Leila's experience. "Just tell them what you've told me. They'll be happy with that."

This was new.

For the better part of her life, Leila was used to being treated as an unpaid-domestic-errand girl Cinderella (even though she was Pearl's natural and only child). She knew that her mother loved her. For Pearl, a single woman with a child to support and a business to run, survival was at the top of her list, not sentimentality. But the war had changed things. There was rationing; factories made rivets for tanks and not for refrigerators; thousands of men had enlisted and were fighting overseas in the South Pacific, western Poland, and Germany, in towns and countries that few in Leila's neighborhood had ever heard of. Men who used to be clerks, janitors, and students were now soldiers. Women—like Leila—who were secretaries, maids, and teachers now worked in factories, and some were also soldiers of a kind. And this brought with it a sea of change for both mother and daughter.

Not that it stopped Pearl from making commitments on her daughter's behalf.

"They want me to give a speech!" Leila wailed.

"No, not a speech exactly," Pearl said unconvincingly as she avoided eye contact. "A few remarks, that's all. What it's like in the army. That's what they want to know," she added quickly as she patted Leila's hair. She stepped back to assess the finished product.

"Do you have a notebook, Lee? You might want to jot down a few things. You know, to gather your thoughts. So you'll remember."

Leila sighed.

So. Not a speech then.

Leila repeated this over and over to herself as she faced the ladies of the Women's Improvement Club of the Pine Street AME Church. She'd discussed the high points of army life: basic training, Admin

School at Ft. Des Moines, and her first assignment at Ft. Riley. A bundle of nerves when she started, Leila began to relax in the familiar surroundings amidst the friendly faces and noted pride on her mother's face. Mostly she answered questions and that was easy. Until she noticed Mrs. Delaney's hand raised. Pearl, who was sitting in the front row, rolled her eyes. Rose-Margo Delaney was a woman of strong opinions who, in her own mind, had concluded that she knew everyone and everything worth knowing. If you knew it yesterday, she knew it two days ago. If you knew Her Majesty Queen Elizabeth, Mrs. Delaney knew Her Majesty's great-aunt. She was the kind of person who worked hard to gain your confidence and then gleefully used whatever you'd told her to plunge a knife into your back. Anyone with the smallest drop of self-preservation avoided her like the plague.

"When it comes to Rose-Margo, I use the *p* word," Leila's mother had once said about her. "Phony."

"It's nice to see one of our own doing so well," the woman cooed; the sound of her voice made Leila's skin crawl. "Part of Mrs. B's initiative," she added as if she was a personal friend of Mrs. Bethune. But when Rose-Margo Delaney began a comment with a sugar cube, she invariably ended it with acid. "It's such a shame though," she added, "that her plan has taken such a dark turn."

Murmurs began in the audience.

There was only one way to deal with the woman and that was head-on. Leila took a deep breath.

"I don't understand what you're talking about, Mrs. Delaney," she said.

The woman giggled.

"Well, you know I'm not one to gossip, but . . ." She paused for dramatic effect. "It's just that, well, you know it's been in the press. How should I put it?"

Put it up your butt sideways, Leila dearly wanted to say.

"I read in the *Pittsburgh Courier* that you . . . girls . . . what do they call you, W . . ."

"Women's Army Corps," Leila said, using as much edge in her voice as she dared. "WACs for short."

"Yes, the WACs. That you girls are really there to . . . entertain, you know, the men. Personally entertain them, you understand."

Leila smiled so broadly that her cheeks began to ache.

"I can't imagine why the *Courier* would print such nonsense!" she said calmly. "I've met some of their reporters, you know, on the base, at Ft. Des Moines and Ft. Oglethorpe too," she added, knowing that mentioning the OTC, which hinted at the combat training she'd received there, was probably off limits. "They've observed some of our activities, the training we've received, and they're familiar with the important work we do."

"Yes, they mentioned that, but . . ."

Leila cut her off.

"Why they would say such things is beyond me. It's false and ridiculous. Our days begin at six in the morning and end at ten at night, and there's work to be done from sunup to past sunset," Leila commented. "I don't know when we'd even have the time to socialize or . . . how did you put it? Entertain? We don't have the time or energy to entertain anyone!"

The murmurs were growing louder.

Mrs. Delaney, feeling that she was about to lose control of her supporters, stepped into the mud—unknowingly—with both feet.

"Yes, I'm sure that's true during the day. But this is . . . um . . . after-the-sun-goes-down entertainment that I'm talking about. And our boys . . ."

Leila felt the top of her head spinning.

"Mrs. Delaney, let me just stop you there. I don't know where this rumor started and, honestly, I don't give a rat's behind." Gasps and shocked expressions followed this statement with one exception: Pearl Branch was grinning from ear to ear. "Our women, those of us who answered Mrs. Bethune's call, are working hard every day, sometimes for over ten hours a day. We barely have the energy to get ourselves ready for lights out at night. Entertaining anyone is out of the picture even when we're off duty. And just to make sure that you understand, we acknowledge that 'your boys,' as you put it, are being entertained because when I was stationed at Ft. Riley, we were reassigned to work on the hospital wards. And I'll tell you, we were run off our feet . . ."

Giving penicillin shots every three hours to your boys who'd contracted . . . um, let me see. How shall I put it? Social diseases? And they certainly didn't get them from me!

Leila had been away from Ft. Riley for at least six weeks, but the experiences she'd had there, good and bad, were fresh in her mind. The rustic barracks with their potbellied stoves, Dr. Lazlo, Rainey Barbour's biscuits, Doro and Hazel, and Leila's first, and she hoped, *last*, assignment as a nurse in a military hospital.

Whether it was due to a shortage of nurses, poor planning, or a logistical error, the majority of Ft. Riley's nursing staff had been reassigned and transferred from the old cavalry outpost weeks before the arrival of qualified replacements. By the time the deficit was discovered, it was too late. Most of the regular nurses were gone. The interim solution was to reassign the remaining female staff—WACs—to the hospital complex until the replacement nurses arrived.

Not soon enough, Leila remembered grumbling to herself as she scurried from pillar to post, wrapping, dispensing, wiping (disgusting), lifting, and jabbing—as in administering penicillin shots to soldiers who'd picked up unfortunate diseases.

"Nelson! Keep still!"

"I don't like needles."

"Well, you'll have to lump it, soldier."

"Didn't you just give me a shot?"

"Yes, Private. And you're due for another one. Every three hours."

"That was too hard!"

"Sorry," she'd said through clenched teeth.

"Can't I take a pill?"

The complaints and whining were endless. Of course, it wasn't just about the shots. The bed making, hospital food (which was prepared by a separate KP crew and not by Rainey's people), bedpan duty, and room temperature ("I'm cold! I thought I told you to get me another blanket!") came under the men's scrutiny and criticism too. Nothing the women did was right even though they worked rotating ten-hour shifts to get the work done, doing their best as substitutes to fill in for trained nurses. As challenging as training was at Ft. Oglethorpe—crawling on her belly, climbing ropes, and wading across shallow streams, Leila felt that she had never worked harder in her life, or felt the worse for it, than when she worked on the ward at the Ft. Riley Hospital.

And now this witch was going to tell her that she and her sister WACs were living lives of luxury and serving as bedmates?

Oh, hell no!

The memories provided the vocabulary needed to correct this lie, once and for all!

". . . giving penicillin shots every three hours to *your* boys who'd contracted . . . um, how shall I put it? Social diseases. Yes, that's it, social diseases. Now our job was not to find out *where* they'd contracted these . . . conditions, just to treat them." Leila ended this comment with a wide grin. "And I can say with confidence that our girls, my sister WACs, were not the source of these conditions. Speaking of that . . ." Now it was Leila's turn to pause for dramatic effect. "My mother told me that your Percy was hospitalized briefly when he was at Ft. Huachuca, Mrs. Delaney. I was sorry to hear that." Leila paused to catch her breath. "I hope that he's better now."

Pandemonium filled the room. Leila's fingers cramped after she shook every hand in the receiving line—including Mrs. Delaney's. Pearl's face glowed with pride. As she kissed Leila on the cheek, she whispered in her ear, "You gave it to her good, baby. That bitch."

THE LETTER V

Spring 1945
Headquarters of the 6888th Central
Postal Directory Battalion
St. Edward's School
Birmingham, England

Dorothy's nose twitched. The room smelled like feet and something else.

She, Leila, and the other women exchanged glances. They didn't know where to look. The geography of the room was not what they were expecting. They had been briefed on the train from Glasgow to Birmingham, their assignment explained, the logistics outlined, and the location identified. They weren't responsible for setting up the quarters, that work was complete. The first contingent of WACs had arrived a month earlier on the *Île de France*, crossing the Atlantic on an irregular course in eleven tense days due to the suspected presence of German U-boats. Racked with seasickness and anxiety, the women had arrived in various states of exhaustion, one of them swearing that she would not return to the States until a bridge was built across the Atlantic. The second group had its own tales of woe from the Atlantic crossing. The worse they were, the more they became a badge of honor. Once they settled in, the battalion was fully staffed with 31 officers and over 800 enlisted women. Their orders were clear: they were a postal unit, charged with processing the mail that had been stockpiled over the many months of the European campaigns. Just recently, several consignments of Christmas mail, including gifts and food, enough to fill six airplane hangars, had been sent back to England from France, following the disarray after the Battle of the Bulge. Now, stockpiled in staging areas across Europe, millions of pieces of mail, bags and bags of them—letters as well as packages—awaited processing. Every piece needed to be sorted, evaluated, repackaged, and redirected to its proper addressee, an American, military or civilian, serving in the European theater. The Commanding Officer Major Adams had designated the only space on the school premises that was large enough to serve as a work area. But even it couldn't hold *all* of the undelivered mail *and* the workspace at the same time, so trucks arrived at intervals and with a roar—there was no other word for the sound—dumped on the gymnasium floor tons of paper, envelopes, boxes, and packages of all sizes.

Dorothy suppressed a sneeze. *Dust. That's what I smell. That and . . .* She and Leila looked at each other, then at the mountain of paper in front of them. They were in a gymnasium, the largest enclosed space in the building. St. Edward's was once a private boys' school, which were called "public schools" in England. Dorothy could never keep that distinction straight. The room smelled of adolescence—stinky toes and sweaty armpits. But the paper mountain had added its own aromas of mold, mildew, rotting food, and . . . In the shadows where the mountain of mail met the wall, scratching scurrying sounds distracted the women. This was followed by the rapid movement of a small dark animal that sent some of the women into shrieks.

"Rats," Dorothy said flatly.

Leila shuddered. *Wonderful. Feet and rats.*

Being in the second unit had its advantages. By the time Dorothy and Leila arrived, the postal unit was fully operational if understaffed. The women only had to attend a brief orientation and step into the flow. The old school building had been refitted and supplied, the barracks furnished. The steam-heating system had been overhauled and, even though it didn't quite meet American expectations of central heating, it worked well enough and often enough to compensate for the chilly damp English spring weather, although Dorothy often wore two sweaters for warmth, Georgia girl that she was.

After unpacking her kit, Dorothy made an appointment at the on-site beauty parlor created exclusively for the women of the unit. Then she reported to the main postal area to receive her work assignment.

"Thank goodness you girls arrived! Thom, I got you over here!" the sergeant shouted, waving a card in the air to get Dorothy's attention. She was grinning. The processing areas were neatly organized in alphabetical order and each "station" was supplied with the necessary index cards, pens, pencils, scissors, and packing materials, including tape, string, and mailing labels.

A large box rested on a table where the sergeant pointed.

"These are yours," the sergeant said, running her hand across the top of the index cards in the file. She gestured to her left at a community of wire baskets near overflowing with letters and small packets. "This is the mail that you're responsible for, men whose last names begin with the letter *V*. Once you've finished these, Thom"—she directed Dorothy's attention to a WAC moving a cart of mail through the door—"Brennan will take them up and move them on for delivery. Then she'll bring you another batch."

"Yes, Sergeant," Dorothy said crisply. The baskets were full but nothing she couldn't handle. She knew what to do and didn't plan to spend much time "prayin' over it," as Big Dad would have said. She'd have these done in no time. The letter *V*. Honestly? How many *V*s could there be? Dorothy picked a letter from one of the baskets. *Lt. Warren Vernon.*

A few weeks later, with her head resting comfortably on a towel-padded shampoo bowl, her eyes closed, and her nostrils inhaling a gentle scent of lavender with vanilla notes, Dorothy chuckled at her own stupidity. How many *V*s were there? Hundreds. Maybe thousands.

"What's so funny, Doro?" Special Services Specialist Glenda Jones asked. "You're not laughing at me, are you?"

Dorothy moved her head slightly, without opening her eyes, and sighed. The hairdresser's fingers gently whirled their way through

Dorothy's damp hair. Glenda's scalp massages were legendary. Among the services specialists—professional hairdressers in civilian life—who populated the Special Services component beauty parlor of the Six Triple Eight, Glenda was the most popular. The women drew cards, tossed coins, and on occasion, nearly came to blows in their quest to have a shampoo, scalp massage, press, and curl with Specialist Jones.

"On my honor and hope not to die, Glen," Dorothy murmured, "I am not laughin' at you!"

Glenda chuckled and continued her work, which could only be defined as divine. And Dorothy, while bemoaning the unexpectedly large amount of mail addressed to soldiers whose surnames began with *V*, including Vincent, Vance, Von Hagen, Vionetti, and hundreds more, thanked her lucky stars that she (A) had made an appointment with Specialist Jones and (B) that their CO, Major Adams, had had the foresight to embed a beauty parlor within the structure of the postal directory unit. Attracting Black nurses as well as Red Cross and other aid workers from across England, it was the second-busiest department on the WAC post. Staffed with beauticians and equipped with pressing combs and Marcel curling irons (imported from France, of course) along with electrical outlets and creatively wired gas lines, the post's beauty parlor elevated the spirits of the women, whose unit motto was "No mail, low morale."

"Negro women and hair, that's all you need to know," Leila commented, running her hands across her freshly pressed ebony hair. "If your hair doesn't look right or feel right, *you* won't feel right. I'm sure that's in the Bible somewhere."

"Leila, make yourself useful and hand me some of those bobby pins," Glenda said.

Leila watched as the hairdresser's nimble fingers worked the curls in Dorothy's hair. Then Leila grinned.

"Say, Glen, see if you can do a roll-up in the front. Like the one Lena Horne has in *Stormy Weather*."

Dorothy snorted.

"Then I'm going to need some Lena Horne hair to make it work!" she said laughing. "And a lot more bobby pins!"

Dorothy raised her hand and formed her fingers into a *V*. The much-needed shampoo, press, and curl was a godsend, just the respite she needed from the busiest department on post and all those darned "Vees."

No one was exactly sure how much mail needed attention, but with at least seven million US personnel actively supporting the war in Europe, the estimates ran in the millions. And six months wasn't a long time. Adams organized the work around a three eight-hour shifts per day, seven days per week schedule. No whining was allowed. The war had been fought all across Europe with personnel shifted from pillar to post and back again for the better part of the last three years, with the result that few American soldiers or civilian-auxiliary personnel had received word from home. The women were determined to change that.

The procedures were simple and owed their efficiency to an ordinary index card filing system. All American personnel serving in Europe, military and civilian, had an address card on file, listing name, serial number, and duty locations. As the duty assignments changed, a change-of-address card was completed and sent to the postal unit. As cards were revised, the postal clerk's job was to examine each piece of mail, identify the individual addressee, and update the delivery address on the mail while noting the processing date and initials of the mail handler. If the letter or package was damaged in some way, it was referred to specialists who repaired (if possible) or repackaged the item, then sent it on its way. Once Dorothy compared the *V*-named soldier with his mail, she quickly readdressed the letter, marking the envelope appropriately, then passed it on to Brennan, whose job it was to take the carts to the loading docks. If the attempted delivery didn't work, the mail was returned to the Six Triple Eight to be checked and processed again.

No one could say that the American GIs were forgotten. The mounds of mail included food packages containing every type of cuisine and goody imaginable, all of which over the past three years had received the undivided attention of mold, mildew, ants, roaches, mice, or rats. In most of the cases, the packaging had disintegrated, leaving a disgusting and smelly mess behind that was handled gingerly and with glove-covered hands by the women.

"Doro, what is this?" one of Dorothy's co-workers asked. The poor girl's eyes were watering. She pointed to a pulpy-paper-and-something-else mound on the worktable. The smell emanating from it was stomach-turning.

Dorothy quickly pinched her nostrils.

"You mean, what *was* that?" she said, wondering how they were ever going to extract a name and address from . . . whatever it was.

Other packages, those containing clothing, usually sweaters for warmth or underwear sent by anxious wives or mothers, required more focused and expert attention. Leila, who could wrap

Christmas gifts like a pro thanks to her seasonal jobs at Elder and Johnson's Department Store in Dayton, unbundled the items, unfolding and discarding mildewed or damaged items and refolding and packaging them for delivery. Her nimble fingers smoothed neat creases into the tissue paper, then repackaged the gift into fresh brown wrapping paper and sent them on their way, with a prayer that Pvt. or Cpl. What's-His-Name was alive and still resident at the last posting noted on his card and would happily unwrap the long-sleeved undershirt or Gruen watch sent for his birthday two years earlier.

The handling could be tedious, and sometimes, especially after several unsuccessful delivery attempts had been made, Dorothy wondered if there was any point. Once a letter had been redirected and returned for thirty days, the final step was to mark it "return to sender." But she hated to do that. All she could think about was how this parent or wife would feel seeing those three words. Often, without making a big deal about it, Dorothy stretched the processing past thirty days, sometimes to forty-five. Knowing that a soldier hadn't heard from home in over a year and sometimes longer pushed her to try just once more. She started a list of the letters and packages that she handled more than once. And at the end of a shift, there were few things—aside from a stroll to a pub in Birmingham or a dinner out—that were more satisfying than noting that a letter that she'd processed two, three, or more times had not yet returned. That, like a homing pigeon, it had finally found its proper home.

Dorothy decided when she first arrived in England that if possible she would make use of the opportunity and travel. France held her heart, but any place she hadn't been (and that was a lot of places) was fair game. So when a three-day leave presented itself, Dorothy took a train to London.

She went prepared. It was spring in the Midlands so she wore her army-issue coat. And it was England so she also brought an umbrella. She tagged along with a trio of Chicago girls who thought that she was overdressed and teased her. They bragged that they were immune to cold and that it was only "a little chilly." Once they stepped off the train at Euston Station, they realized their mistake. Black umbrellas were ubiquitous. And despite the date on the calendar, it wasn't chilly. It was cold.

But if she was prepared for the weather, Dorothy was not prepared for the vibrant yet ancient city that had survived the Iceni, Saxons, and Romans. It sprawled across a vast landscape with architecture that, in many places, would have been as familiar to Henry VIII in the 1500s as it was to Winston Churchill now. The city was bursting with people, cars, trams, horses, and fog. Dorothy couldn't believe that she was seeing with her own eyes the sights—the Thames, St. Paul's—that she had read about.

The noise was unrelenting, the smell of coal fires and gasoline even more so. The boulevards were jammed with people. Where were they all going, Dorothy wondered. There was so much to see that she didn't know where to look. As she'd promised Leila and Hazel, she paid close attention to what the women were wearing, their shoes and cloth coats held with gloved hands. Red lipstick and some stockinged legs but not many because nylons were hard to find. And uniforms. Everywhere, there were uniforms, as if the military forces of every Allied force had descended on the old capital. The dark khaki of the Australians, deep blue for the RAF, sand-colored khaki for the Indian Army, and olive drab for the Yanks. Some of them did a double take when they passed Dorothy and her friends.

The skyline was clear and open, no longer populated by barrage balloons. At ground level, there were brick buildings, confusing street signs, and sandbags. Bobbies stood on many corners and in the intersections. Dorothy had expected to be awestruck by the usual tourist spots of the city—Buckingham Palace, the historic bridges, and the Tower of London, an unassuming structure despite its ominous history—but it was the relics of the present and recent past that left an imprint on her.

Craters the size of city blocks marked the spots where bombs had done their work too well. With the war in Europe reportedly heading to a close, the city was bustling with construction noise and many buildings were wrapped in scaffolding like gargantuan holiday packages. But the rehabilitated shared space with the injured. Shells of buildings yet to be renovated or demolished were silhouetted against the gray sky: there was one that had a wall complete with not a brick out of place, another wall with barely a brick tower left but cradling the outline of the window of a house where, Dorothy imagined, a mother might have glanced out at a night sky before drawing the shade and kissing her child good night.

Before . . . She had not realized that life and death lived so close together. There was no way to tell if the bomb that had leveled this building left one soul to tell the story. Dorothy felt a chill across her shoulders unrelated to the damp London dusk. She'd pushed these thoughts away, but they could not and would not remain invisible. This war was not yet over either in Europe or in the East. The life of a moment was all that you had. Death, mercurial as to timing, was never far away. Dorothy wiped away the tears with the back of her hand and walked on quickly to catch up with her friends.

Down the Pub

Arm in arm, they walked down the street, talking, cracking jokes, giggling, and breathing in gulps of the Birmingham air, which smelled faintly of graphite and methane depending on which direction your nose was pointed. But off post, at least, the breeze was free of the aromas of rotting food, rat poop, or mildew. The atmosphere of the gym was close and could be overwhelming even when the doors to the outside were open. The trio—Dorothy, Hazel, and Leila—said "Hello" and "Good afternoon" to passing citizens and were cordially addressed in turn. On occasion they were accosted by small packs of juveniles, eight to twelve years old, who cheekily pestered all Americans for the goodies that they knew were in their shopping baskets and made special requests for oranges, chocolate, and chewing gum.

"Any gum, chum?" they asked, their hands outstretched with grubby palms open in anticipation.

This pub night out was a gift from heaven. It had been a tough two weeks. A convoy of army trucks delivered a Mt. Everest–size mountain of mail that had been stockpiled from the early days of the Battle of the Bulge. Added to the mail already in process, the women quickly became overwhelmed, working until they were near dead on their feet in the damp and, sometimes, dim conditions because of the blackout curtains. With three shifts on the schedule rotation, the old boys' school turned postal service ran almost twenty-four hours a day, with one group of women asleep, one off duty, and one on duty. Even the beauty salon operated from sunup to past sundown. For days, there was little time for socializing. If there were hours to spare, sleep was at the top of the list of preferred activities.

It didn't help that the unit became a quasi-tourist stop for military brass.

"Let's face it," one of the sergeants grumbled, "they've never seen so many Negro women in one place before. And in uniform too."

"It's like we're zoo animals," Dorothy commented after coming face-to-face with a startled lieutenant colonel on her way from the showers. She'd been modestly covered, wearing a pink bathrobe that was as large and bulky as her army-issue coat, her hair wrapped with a scarf, and arctics on her feet because the building was never warm enough. But still. Didn't these officers have better things to do?

"Apparently not," Leila said. The word was that a colonel had been dissatisfied with the conditions around the post and informed their CO, Major Adams, that he would assign a white male first lieutenant to show her how to run the battalion.

"No kidding!"

"What?"

"And what did she say to that?" Dorothy asked, wondering with a tiny amount of guilt if the irritable colonel was the same officer that *she* had nearly run into. "I hope she told him 'bugger off,' as the Brits say."

Leila, whose fill-in work in the secretarial pool afforded a convenient front-row seat to all kinds of juicy tidbits, lowered the volume of her voice again.

"Well, not quite but close. Lizzie said that Jean said that Lieutenant Hill told her that Major Adams said, you know, in that calm polite way of hers, 'Over my dead body, sir.'"

There was laughter and murmurs of approval all round. Major Adams was not one to put up with any foolishness, official or not, even if her retort could get her court-martialed. For several days, the story spread and the women were on pins and needles, their admiration for the CO balanced with the chance that the unit could be in jeopardy. Would the Six Triple Eight be disbanded? The major disciplined? Or worse?

The rumors swirled and there were several tall tales that circulated, but the truth of what did or did not occur behind the scenes was never clear. What *was* clear?

Major Adams was not reprimanded. And no male white first lieutenant was assigned to the Six Triple Eight. Ever.

*   *   *

It was Wednesday nearing dusk and the women, their shifts completed and off duty until Friday, had decided to do some shopping, walk around the town square, and get some exercise, then top off their much-looked-forward-to evening out with a pub dinner and drinks.

"Fish and potato sticks for me," Leila said, her mouth watering at the suggestion. "I just love those potato things, especially with vinegar."

Dorothy snorted.

"Chips, girl," she said. "They're called 'chips.'"

Leila frowned.

"Not what I think of when I think of chips, like Mikesell's at home, but okay. If you say so."

"I do," Dorothy added with certainty in her voice. "Me? I think I'll have . . ."

"Steak and kidney pie?" Hazel piped in, suppressing a giggle in her throat.

Dorothy gulped.

"I like steak. And I like pie. But I don't like kidneys of any kind or in any way. And I am definitely not thinking about having them in a pie." She shuddered. "Whatever that looks like."

"What *does* that look like?" Leila asked, her frown deepening.

Hazel chuckled.

"It looks like I'll be the adventurous one then. The captain I met, you know the one I told you about; he's Canadian, name is Anderson. He said that those pie things reminded him of home. His mother's from England." She stopped and it was her turn to frown. "Can't remember exactly where . . . begins with *S*. Something-shire?"

"Lots of shires around," Dorothy said.

"Be careful, you and that captain," Leila said.

"We're just acquaintances," Hazel said coolly.

"Uh-huh," Dorothy commented. "Just be careful like the child said," she added.

"I can hear you," Leila growled. "And I am not a child. In fact, I've actually *had* a child!"

Giggles, then laughter accompanied this remark as the women continued down the street toward The Bell, stopping for a moment to greet a woman who sometimes helped out at the post.

Hazel stopped and looked over her shoulder as the woman waved and walked on.

"You know, it's strange, not having to step aside when white folks walk on the same sidewalk."

Dorothy glanced back and nodded.

"I know. I'd darned near be walking in the street all the time if this was Dublin, Georgia. But this is not Georgia."

It was a sentiment they spoke of often and none of them was yet so blasé as to take it for granted. In Laurens County, Dorothy didn't have to imagine the consequences if she had not stepped aside or even into the street to avoid passing directly next to a white man or woman when she was a child. It was tragically familiar for her family and their neighbors. For Hazel, born and raised in Kansas City, the "rule" was not as pronounced, but the precaution was the same, especially where her Mississippi-born father was concerned. He stepped aside, removed his hat, and lowered his gaze, especially when a white woman was near to passing by. Old fears were the last to fade away. Dayton had different customs but only just. In many areas of the city, Black and white people lived in close proximity, although not in the same neighborhoods. But there was often an invisible yet palpable sense of wariness that permeated the interactions of the citizens, and unwritten rules were passed from parent to child, friend to friend to prevent an unfortunate incident. "Make sure you drive real slow through such-and-such area."

The Bell was buzzing, as usual, as it had for nearly three hundred or more years. Its original structure dated from the 1700s or 1800s depending on who told the story, and over the centuries, it had earned its place as a popular watering hole. It closed for a short time after the Luftwaffe roared through Birmingham's factories and proximity to coal made it an attractive target. And, like the rest of the country, the old manufacturing city hunkered down, especially after a four-day onslaught of bombing in November 1940.

Over the next couple years, as the war and the Germans shifted attention to the east, the city gathered its resources, both physical and emotional, and made a start toward rebuilding the homes, factories, and businesses decimated during the Blitz even though they sometimes had to do it in between sporadic air raids. The Bell was no exception. Now renovated, the timber and white-stucco public house not far from the old city center operated at full capacity, its tables, bar, and parlors bursting with men and women, locals and military wearing the uniforms of Britain and its colonial and former colonial outposts. Its walls vibrated with laughter and conversation with inflections from as far afield as San Francisco, Kingston, Auckland, and Halifax.

"There's no place to sit!" Dorothy shouted. The noise level in the pub was deafening. "We'll have to stand at the bar!" She felt a tug on her arm. Hazel gestured to the left.

"Ronnie's got a table, over there. See?"

Over the heads of the crowd, an arm moved back and forth like the pendulum of an upside-down clock.

"At least he's tall," grumbled Dorothy as she and Leila maneuvered through the crowd, each holding the other's hand to keep from getting lost. The tall man in the distinct greenish-brown khaki uniform of the Canadian Army smiled and pulled out chairs.

"Have a seat, ladies," the officer said, smiling. "In case you don't know . . ." He leaned across the table. "I'm Captain Ronald Mackenzie Anderson, First Canadian Army, at your service. I'm Ronald to my mum, Old Son to my dad, and Ron to my mates. But Private Diggs, here, for some unfathomable reason, calls me 'Ronnie.'" He winked at Hazel, who blushed. "What'll you have?"

Dorothy knew about Hazel's "friend" and had expressed an opinion—without being asked for it—and had gotten an earful in response. Leila had seen them together once and that was enough to send her heart pounding, more from anxiety than anything else, but wisely, she said nothing. This was the first time that either of them had met the captain in the flesh and they were promptly won over. Ronnie had the unreserved likeability of a friendly Labrador but taller. He was charming, well-mannered, and funny. And he was madly in love with Hazel—gazing at her with open affection when she wasn't looking. Dorothy and Leila exchanged glances, not knowing whether to be delighted or dismayed.

He turned his attention to Hazel.

"Are you hungry?"

Hazel's answer was a smile.

Oh, dear, Dorothy thought. *She looks at him as if he was a cinnamon bun just out of the oven.*

Ronnie took their food and drinks orders with the aplomb of a practiced waiter, bowed gallantly, then made his way through the throng toward the bar. Dorothy remembered her and the girls' first pub visit when they sat at the table and waited. And waited. And waited for table service until a helpful Royal Navy ensign informed them that orders for both food and drink were placed at the bar.

"I'm starving," Hazel commented. She stood up, then craned her neck so that she could see better. "It's no good, he'll be a while," she shouted as she sat down. "Three people deep over there."

"But at least I'm off my feet," Dorothy said, pushing off a shoe, then rubbing her ankle. "Honestly, what I wouldn't give for a pair of army-issue shoes that actually fit!"

"Me too," Leila said. She stretched out one foot and wiggled her toes. "My feet are too long and narrow. And Doro, yours are too short and wide!"

As they waited for Ronnie's return, the women chatted and people watched, enjoying the lively atmosphere of the pub, feeling as if they and the other patrons hadn't a care in the world even if there was a war on. There were lots of pubs in the city, and it seemed that in the old city center, there was at least one on every corner. Everyone had their favorites, either because their father and their father's father drank there, their cousin's in-laws pulled the pints, or because that's where they went every Thursday after work, rain or shine, winter or summer, and had since God wore short pants. The names were as original and ancient as the buildings, with the proprietor of one noteworthy establishment, The Poacher's Point, swearing on a stack of Bibles and a 1689 edition of the Book of Common Prayer (interesting considering the name of the pub)

that it had been in business since the late 1300s. Although, by looking at the building, Dorothy doubted it. 1600? That was possible.
Few of Birmingham's most popular pubs had grown up in any
century remotely close to the twentieth.

The Bell was special. Dorothy always enjoyed an evening at the
old pub. There was nothing like it "back home," she mused. Not the
Harlem clubs, Atlanta's after-hours spots, or the joint situated down
the dirt road that ran parallel to Old Man McGuffie's farm, near the
banks of the Oconee. It operated in a run-down farmhouse, had no
fixed name or ownership, and was open (sometimes and occasionally) depending on whether or not the proprietor was in the pokey.
The combination of drinks, as in whiskey, ale, or pints—no custom
cocktails, thank you—and basic brown and white food was familiar
and, in a strange way, comforting. "Nothing fancy," she heard Big
Dad's voice in her head. Potatoes, peas (not her favorite vegetable),
meat, some beef, pork or lamb, chicken, and—God save us—meat
pies, which Dorothy could look at but not consume. The food was
plain and barely seasoned, but it was hot and nourishing. The fire
was warm and comforting, there was no central heating, the chairs
were comfy, and the company friendly. But the noise could be a
presence and, once everyone had at least two pints in them, the din
rose to earsplitting level.

Dorothy looked at her watch: nine thirty. They'd eaten and
she'd been here an hour and a half. And her temples were pounding. For all the things that Dorothy enjoyed about The Bell, she
could only enjoy it in short doses of time and nearly always left
with a headache. Most nights, you couldn't hear the conversation
within two feet of your elbow. But this evening was an exception.

There was a short lull between the end of one song, played by a group of local musicians, and the beginning of the next one. It lasted only a few seconds, not even a minute. But that was long enough.

"... thought this was for whites only ..."

Dorothy's shoulders rose, but she resisted the urge to turn her head. No need to see where that came from.

She'd seen them come in half an hour ago; their table was in the corner, barely six feet away. Four GIs, barely old enough to shave, early twenties at best, and already slightly "pissed," as the Brits liked to say. She'd watched as they surveyed the surroundings, clocking the empty table, then once seated, noticing the three WACs sitting close by. One of the boys—because he looked so young that Dorothy couldn't think of him as anything but—locked eyes with her and stood up as if preparing to leave, his face contorted with disgust. Dorothy looked away; her attention had been diverted by Leila's touch on her sleeve.

Ronnie had told a joke, complete with sound effects and mimicry. Leila was giggling and Hazel choked on her drink, her hands shaking as she laughed.

"... don't do it at home and I'm sure not gonna do it here ..."

Before any of them could think to respond, the soldier was at Hazel's elbow, his thin pimpled face scarlet with rage.

"What d'you think you're doin'? Sittin' up here like you belong in a decent place like this? Go to the colored section. Better yet, find you a colored club!"

Hazel stood up and rounded on him.

"I've got as much right to be here as you do, Private!" she

countered in a voice loud enough to be heard over the din. "No colored section here!"

Startled, the soldier stepped back but was soon surrounded by his mates, who had stood up to see what was happening.

"There's no colored club, it's one club!" Leila shouted.

The background chatter was now subdued as the patrons at the surrounding tables took notice of the situation. Out of the corner of her eye, Dorothy noticed that some of them were standing.

"In this man's army, whites and coloreds serve in separate units, at home and here," the soldier spat out, reenergized by what he assumed was solidarity coming from his mates and the other patrons.

"No separate spaces *here*, old man," Ronnie chimed in, using a calm tone as he pulled himself to his full height. "We're all pushing Herr Hitler against the ropes together, y'understand."

The young man downed his pint in one gulp, slamming the glass mug on the table.

"That may be, but we got rules when it comes to coloreds. You let them out with good white people *here*, but in America, we keep our niggers in their place."

"That's an ugly word," an Australian Army soldier exclaimed.

Emboldened by the energy and the ale, the private grabbed another pint from his table, poured it down his gullet, and wiped his mouth with the back of his hand. With watery blue eyes, he looked around the table, taking in the tall Canadian, a stocky red-headed man wearing the deep khaki uniform of the Kiwis, and a group of RAF pilots standing to his left, fury imprinted on their faces. He grinned. Every white man in the room was on his side. Filled with liquor-fueled bravado—and ignoring a warning from one of his drinking buddies, "Ernie, you don't want to do that . . ." He glanced at Dorothy, whose head barely reached the Kiwi's shoulder. He chuckled as he caught her eye.

"The nigras here . . ."

A fist that felt like a rock connected with his jaw and sent him reeling backwards into the embrace of his friends. He was too stunned and too drunk to retaliate but wouldn't have been able to anyway, since he was instantly set upon by, among many others, the barkeep, four Canadians, three RAF officers, two Kiwis, three Royal Navy ensigns, and one Australian. As well as three enraged US Army WACs.

The Yankee boys were thrown out and told by The Bell's owner that they were welcome to take their drinking business elsewhere. They were ungently and unceremoniously escorted away by a bobby and two off-duty MPs, whether to a Birmingham jail or a brig on their post, no rumor ever specified. Although it was noted by an anonymous observer that the young GIs, especially the one named "Ernie," were a bit the worse for wear upon arrival.

* * *

"We'll walk you back to St. Edward's," Ronnie said, his face, frown and all, half in shadows from the pub's outside lamps. The other men nodded, murmuring their assent.

"You guys were great, truly. Thank you so much," Dorothy

said. Glancing up at Teddy, the Kiwi, she winced. His cheek, once just slightly swollen and looking as if someone had applied a few swipes of coral rouge, was now turning purple with yellow highlights. "Teddy, you've got to get that seen to."

The Kiwi grinned and bowed dramatically.

"By your orders, ma'am," he said with the last word sounding like "mum."

"But I wonder . . ." The New Zealander paused, glanced at Ronnie and the other men, then continued. "I don't know much about the States, ma'am," he said haltingly. "Just what's in the papers and on the newsreels. But . . . those boys, I mean, they're from a place called Indiana, they said. Indiana is in the north of your country. That's right, isn't it? I thought that . . . well . . . during the Civil War between the states . . ."

For a moment, it was quiet. The four men, New Zealander, Canadian, and British, seemed embarrassed. And the three women, wearing the khaki uniforms of the United States Armed Forces, were silent too, listening to the levity coming from the pub behind them, laughter, the buzz of conversation, and in the background, boogie-woogie music.

"I thought . . . well, we all thought. That those words the boys used, what they said, we thought that was just something that only came from . . . where the slavery was, I think." Ted swallowed. "The Southern states."

Hazel's lips were pressed together in anger. Leila's cheeks were damp despite the handkerchief balled up in her hand. Dorothy's face was dry. Her features had hardened into a marble-like mask.

She looked down at her bruised left hand and wiggled her fingers. Two nails broken and her hand was throbbing like nobody's business. She must have put every pound of her weight and inch of her height into that punch.

"No," Dorothy said, her voice low with inflections of the red Georgia soil embedded within its vowels. "The United States."

*   *   *

It was a long night. By the time the women reached the post, it was past curfew. They steeled themselves for another confrontation—this one with their lieutenant. They were exhausted and a little down, but they knew the rules and had assumed that there would be consequences for being late even though they had their story and battle scars to back it up. When they saw that Lieutenant Hill was waiting for them, they knew that they were in trouble. Had a complaint about the altercation at The Bell already reached the CO?

But the lieutenant looked sad rather than angry.

"Ladies. You share quarters with Private Barbour, don't you? She's one of your circle?"

"Yes, ma'am," Dorothy, Hazel, and Leila replied in unison.

The lieutenant sighed.

"Good. Come with me. I'm afraid she's had some bad news."

It had taken some time for the hostilities from what came to be called "the Battle of the Bulge" to wind down. And it took even longer for the army to release the names of the injured and missing in action. But the names of those who died in the conflicts came in their own good time. And if one of those names was a loved one, that time was always too soon.

Rainey was curled up in the fetal position on the floor of the showers. She had cried herself out of tears. She had wailed until her voice gave out. She looked as if she was dying. Rainey fought and scratched her friends when they tried to move her to a bed. She shouted at Dorothy and thrashed into Leila, nearly knocking her down. But somehow, using their combined strength and all the soothing words they knew, Dorothy, Hazel, Leila, and Lieutenant Hill managed to settle Private Lorraine "Rainey" Barbour into a bed in the infirmary and stayed with her until the shot the doctor administered took effect.

It had happened before, of course, the notification of death by war. Men injured, missing, gone from the world. They could have been used to it. But that wasn't possible. Whole families had died right there in Birmingham during the Blitz. The American Navy had nearly been wiped out at Pearl Harbor. Planes were shot down, pilots dead or captured after bombing raids over Germany. Men were blown up or gunned down. No one was immune from the human devastation even at St. Edward's School. One WAC's older brother, another's husband, the neighbor's boy from down the street. And now Rainey Barbour's cousin. They'd been raised together by their grandmother and were the same age. They'd grown up like twins. Rainey was tough as nails, blunt and irreverent. She blew out the smoke from her Chesterfields like a smokestack at an iron forge and cursed like the proverbial sailor to the delight of her sister WACs but to the dismay of her devout Methodist grandmother back home. But when she spoke about Kenny, read out from the one letter she'd received from him over a year ago, her gritty cigarette-sanded voice was smooth and melodic. He was the soft side of her nature. And now he was gone.

It took a while for the drug to work.

"She's fighting it," the doctor observed in a somber voice, shaking his head. "This hit her hard."

The women stood around her bed, murmured the most comforting words they knew, and held her hands until she drifted off. And Dorothy wondered yet again about life, death, and war. It wasn't just Kenny who'd been killed in that bomb blast. But in a way, Rainey had died too.

NO MAIL, LOW MORALE

April 11–12, 1945
Headquarters of the 6888th Central
Postal Directory Battalion
St. Edward's School
Birmingham, England

Dorothy couldn't sleep. After six weeks working second shift from three in the afternoon to eleven at night, she was transferred to first. She'd welcomed the change, figuring that she would finally catch up with the sleep she'd lost getting used to English time. She was wrong. Once adjusted to the time change, when she was reassigned, she had to adjust again. She did, but tonight sleep wouldn't come. It wasn't the snoring (Evelyn, two beds over, was notorious). Betty T. (All the Bettys were identified by first name and surname initial) turned over and over through the night like a top yet woke up bright-eyed and alert in the morning. Unfathomable. Annie had allergies and sneezed. A lot. But most nights, these sounds blended into one long whoosh of nothingness. Dorothy had become so accustomed to them that she blocked them out and slept. But not tonight.

It was four a.m. The gymnasium was lit up, humming with activity as a skeletal crew took on the overflow and loose ends. Yawning, Dorothy made her way over to the coffee station. The sergeant in charge, Mary Wilkes, looked up.

"Thom! What're you doin' here?"

Laughter followed this remark. Dorothy yawned again, then took a sip of coffee and coughed.

"This is awful," she said, pulling a face. "How do you drink this stuff?"

Wilkes chuckled.

"I'm used to it," she said, sliding her glasses onto her nose. "The question is, why are you here? You're not due to report until eight, at which time *I'll* be taking a long shower!"

Dorothy nodded and made her way over to the table, where another PFC was working. The letter *V* was prominently displayed. The WAC smiled at Dorothy.

"Doro, how you doin'?"

"I'm good, Catherine, thanks."

"You're still workin' that boy, aren't you?" the sergeant called over. "How long has it been?"

Dorothy shrugged.

Sergeant Wilkes shook her head.

"Dorothy, thirty days. That's s'posed to be it." Her tone of voice and expression betrayed any belief she held in Dorothy's obedience to the rule. "*And* he's an *S*." She bit her lip to keep from smiling. "Aren't there enough *V*s to keep you busy?"

"Yes, ma'am, Sergeant," Dorothy answered, taking another sip of the disgusting but hot coffee. "There are. Annie needed a little help, that's all."

"Uh-huh," Wilkes chuckled and returned her attention to the stack of papers on her desk.

Catherine opened a file folder and pulled out an envelope with two index cards attached and slid them toward Dorothy.

"Here you go."

1LT RANDALL B SMITH, SERIAL# . . .

It was weeks ago, she'd wrapped up the *V*s for the day but Annie was swamped with *S*s, Smiths to be specific. Lots of Johns and Jameses. Roberts and Bobs. And then this soldier.

An Ohio boy, stationed at Forts Huachuca, Benjamin Harrison, and Oglethorpe before shipping out. Saw action in Normandy and in the Ardennes, Belgium in December 1944.

Dorothy read the notations on the address-change cards, and there were many. She had exceeded the regulation thirty days *by* thirty days. This Lieutenant Smith's mail included, in particular, a thick envelope of light pastel blue that bore the initials of Mrs. J. S. Smith in a flowery hand in the top left corner along with the return address. Was this "Mrs. Smith" his mother writing with the gossip from home? Or his wife writing to tell him of their baby's first steps? It didn't matter. Since November 1944, Mrs. Smith's letter had bounced from pillar to post and back again. And Dorothy had exhausted every address change submitted by the lieutenant—the last one sent over just a month before the beginning of the campaign in the Ardennes in mid-December. Since then, nothing. It was now April. The rumor was that the Six Triple Eight was moving over to France soon, and Major Adams had given orders to begin wrapping up Birmingham operations.

But where would that leave Lieutenant Smith?

"Doro?"

Catherine's voice broke into Dorothy's reverie. She looked down. Catherine held a rumpled watermarked ecru index card between her fingers.

"It came in soaked, but I dried it out," she said, pursing her lips. "Sort of. It's dated February something, hard to tell for sure. But it's definitely from *R*- or *B*-something Smith. Maybe you'll have better luck reading the serial number than I have. Worth a try, though."

The card was damp in places but the handwriting was firm, near perfect, and familiar, Dorothy thought, feeling envious. In school, her marks in penmanship were always low. "Looks like a mosquito skated on the paper," she remembered one teacher's comment. The ink that Smith used—whether *R* or *B*, it was hard to tell— hadn't run too much and most of the information was legible if a little fuzzy. Dorothy pressed the paper as flat and smooth as she could, careful not to scratch or tear it further, then took up her magnifying glass and leaned over to get a close look.

LT-something-SMITH. No ambiguity there. He'd written his last name with confidence in each pen stroke, forming the letters with care. Only the first name initial was in question. The top of the roman letter was clear; it was the bottom half that would make the difference, and Dorothy couldn't tell if it was open, or rounded and closed. But the location name sounded familiar and she compared it with the last change-of-address card this Smith had submitted. A small area in the Ardennes. Her Smith (Dorothy felt as if this soldier was a family member) had been part of the Battle of the Bulge, assigned to an obscure forested area (Dorothy had looked it up) in Belgium. Not that there weren't thousands of Smiths, Bobbies, Robbies, Bobs, and Roberts, but she knew his handwriting. And she knew where he'd been. The new card, likely completed at the end of what had been a drawn-out and bloody campaign on a makeshift lap desk balanced across his knees, told a story about a man who, despite his surroundings—and they had been grim—had the presence of mind to complete a form neatly so that someone else could read it.

The serial number was wiped out by moisture, but his new assignment location was legible and also familiar: Ramitelli AFB in Italy, close to Mt. Vesuvius, which still belched and bubbled even now, and which was not far from the city of Naples. Dorothy sat back in her chair. Ramitelli. She knew that name well. It was the base of operations for the 332nd Airborne Fighter Division, the group of Negro pilots and support crew known as the "Tuskegee Airmen."

There was no decision to be made. Dorothy was willing to take a chance. She noted the file card with the name "RANDALL" and the lieutenant's serial number. Then she readdressed the pale blue envelope with the APO of Ramitelli and sent it on its way, praying that the messages it contained were happy ones and that she wouldn't see it cross her desk again.

A commotion at the front of the gym caught her attention. Conversation in low voices was punctuated by cries of "Oh my God!" and "Oh, no!" and by sobbing. The rapid tip-tap sound of running footsteps echoed in the hall, leaving an ominous impression. Something horrible had happened. She and Catherine stood up at the same time.

"What's going on?" Dorothy called out as she sprinted toward the main registration table. Her first thought was of something dreadful, another sustained bombing by the Luftwaffe or a reversal of the gains made during the Battle of the Bulge. Sergeant Wilkes was dabbing her eyes, as was one of the tech specialists who worked as a post telephone operator. Dorothy's breath caught in her throat. When there was any news, good or bad, the telephone operators with their many connections, including those which snaked their way to 10 Downing Street or Chequers, got wind of it first. Next to the operators in London, the women who staffed the telephone bank at the 6888th in Birmingham were some of the best-informed people in England.

"What's happened?" Dorothy asked.

The operator, who didn't have a hankie, wiped away tears with the back of her hand.

"President Roosevelt is dead."

* * *

He was the only president they had ever known. He was FDR, there was no need to add his surname. He had been president since 1933. Thirteen years. "That's a long way," Sergeant Wilkes said. For many Americans, it was Roosevelt who, like a conjurer pulling a rabbit from a top hat, reset the American economy and, with political savvy, patience, and aplomb, brought the country's Negro citizens along for the ride. Once the country joined the Allies in the war, Roosevelt pulled out every stop to push back hard on the Axis powers and boost American morale to its highest levels. Across Europe and into the Pacific theater, Yanks of every stripe were everywhere. Mrs. Roosevelt and her "best friend" Mrs. Bethune had been fierce advocates for the Negro pilots and the inclusion of Negro women into the WACs. And now, monumental change had taken place again, overnight.

The sniffling went on for some time. Both of Dorothy's hankies were damp by the time she returned to her station. She picked up an oversize envelope that looked as if it had been in the trenches in Belgium during the Battle of the Bulge. The addressee's name and posting were difficult to read even after she dabbed away fresh tears.

It was that radio address that had brought her to this table stacked with mailbags. It was the sound of his voice, the concise, grave words he used: "A date which will live in infamy." FDR was the reason that she was standing in a cavernous boys' gym, squinting to make out the faded script on the envelope.

Corporal something illegible *V*. Was that an *a*?

A man whom she had never met and would never know was the reason she was sending on Corporal Vann's mail.

A new president. Would there also be a new agenda?

The new man was not well-known. And the war, while nearing its end in Europe, still raged in the Pacific, presenting new challenges. When would the troops come home? Or would they be sent to the Pacific? And what about the Negro troops? When their missions were complete, would they be called home too? Or would they have to wait until all of the white military personnel returned to the States?

Roosevelt's death in Warm Springs, Georgia, was officially announced later that morning. The battalion's flag was lowered to half-mast. The US Army based throughout Europe followed its protocols to the letter in recognition of the death of its commander in chief and the women of the 6888th were no exception. The service was brief and simple but impactful. The opening hymn—Hazel, who played the piano, chose "A Mighty Fortress Is Our God"—was sung with fervor and genuine emotion. The 6888th's chaplain led the women in the Lord's Prayer and Major Adams spoke, giving a heartfelt eulogy. And then the postal directory battalion returned to its usual energetic pace with an additional mission to fulfill.

The telephone operators of the 6888th received two communications over the twenty-four-hour period of April 11 and 12. One concerned the death of President Roosevelt. The other contained orders confirming the transfer of the 6888th from Birmingham, England, to Rouen in Normandy, France.

FLAUBERT'S BED

May 1945
Caserne Tallandier
Rouen, France

May brought warmer weather (Dorothy didn't have to wear her arctics in the gymnasium anymore), Leila's birthday (the women celebrated at The Bell with Ronnie and a dozen or more of his friends), and VE Day on the eighth. The people of Birmingham, residents and military, celebrated in the streets, in the pubs, everywhere. Kisses, hugs, and dancing went on beyond the wee hours. Rumors swirled that the angry little man had escaped to Spain or to parts unknown on a U-boat. One of the 6888 operators whispered that the fiend had died by his own hand in Berlin. But nobody really cared. The celebrations were a welcome release, and Dorothy had a monstrous hangover the next day. But even that didn't diminish her enthusiasm for the anticipated transfer of the unit to France. No headache or twirly stomach could do *that*.

From the day, almost from the moment that the order was given, Pfc. Dorothy Thom thought, spoke, and dreamed en français. *Finally!* She remembered what her grandfather had said about her double major of English literature and French. This would be the first opportunity to actually use it. She was beyond excited.

Even better, the 6888th was going to Rouen, the city of Joan of Arc and Gustave Flaubert. To prepare herself, Dorothy spoke to anyone who would listen in French, reread her dog-eared copy of *Madame Bovary*, and daydreamed about sun-swept fields in Provence and Rouen's street of the clock while plotting to find a way to get inside of l'Hôtel-Dieu, the hospital complex where Flaubert, whose *père* was a doctor, was born and spent his early childhood years. The short notice meant that the women were expected to be ready to leave in a matter of days—Major Adams had gone ahead to oversee the preparations for the post. And it didn't take much longer than a few days before Dorothy's closest, Leila and Hazel, were fed up with their friend's *"en français s'il vous plait."*

"You know what you can do with that en français?" Leila barked. Dorothy blew her a raspberry.

"Leila, behave! Now, Dorothy!" Hazel nudged her Francophile friend as they settled into their seats on the train for the trip overland to the Dover coast. "They are not just going to let you come into the place to look around! It's a hospital!"

Leila rolled her eyes.

"And if you tell *me* to en français it, I'll pop you!" Hazel added in a low growl. "It's a busy place and the people there are sick and trying to recuperate. It's not an exhibit at Madame Tussauds!"

"O ye of little faith, I'll sort it somehow," Dorothy countered in English for a change, her excitement barely contained. She'd wanted to go abroad and now she had. Her dream had come true. And reading the works of Flaubert, de Maupassant, and Colette in French had only stoked the flames of her excitement. She couldn't wait until she stepped onto French soil.

The battalion traveled by train, first to London, then to Dover, and then on to Calais. But first, they had to cross a strait of water that had a dubious reputation. The English Channel was known for many things, including variable weather conditions. With the channel, one never really knew. In 1066, William the Conqueror had to put off his invasion of Britain by a month to wait for calm winds and an even calmer sea. Dorothy studied the horizon with trepidation. It was May and the weather was mild, the breeze light. But a light breeze on land could shapeshift into a gale on sea in a matter of minutes and neither Dorothy, Leila, nor Hazel—whose Atlantic crossing sent her to bed for a week—wanted a repeat of that experience. The water was deep green with brown edges glinting like bronze in the sunlight, swooshing against the hull of the boat in a deliberate rhythm like the largo movement of a symphony. Was that a good omen or a bad one?

Dorothy closed her eyes for a moment and sent prayers of supplication to the gods of the sea, whatever their names were.

"What are you doing?" Leila asked.

"Shush. Praying for a smooth crossing if you really want to know. At the moment, I'm asking for mercy from the goddess of the seas."

Leila smiled.

"I didn't know there was a goddess of the sea."

"You mean 'the god of the sea,' right? Poseidon?" Hazel asked with a smirk.

Dorothy shrugged.

"I'm not fooling around with him," she said sharply. "Going straight to the top. To Gaia, the grandmother of all gods, land, sea, and air," she added. "From one female to another, even if she is a goddess. Lady Gaia, please send us calm seas and no whitecap waves, thank you and amen!"

Whether Gaia or her grandson was listening was anyone's guess but there was no guessing about the conditions of the channel when the women of the 6888th made their crossing. The lovely May weather held and the waves decided to forgo wearing their whitecaps.

The train ride across southwestern France from Calais to Rouen was as lovely as it was disturbing. The vistas were green and lush, the fields glowing with the promise of growing crops and flowers and bountiful harvests. Dorothy imagined the birdsong drowned out by the sound of the train. The land looked hopeful and defiant as if boasting of its resilience after the long violent desolation of wars. France had not fully recovered from the desecration of its lands in World War I, and now its landscape was scorched again. Against the bucolic backdrop of forests, valleys, and fertile fields, the imprints of conflict and tragedy were everywhere, the geography scarred by the bones of conflict, bombing, and death. Houses and whole villages were in ruins, the remains imprinted in silhouette against the sky; barns charred and roofless; cars left overturned on the side of the roads, in pieces as if taken apart by giant fingers; tanks left where they fell, broken as if by a giant's fist. In the British countryside and in Birmingham, the bombs had made their marks as well, but the Brits emerged from taking cover and moved quickly to erase the evidence, even if it meant that there were empty lots and massive craters in the earth left to wait until supplies and workers were free to repair or repopulate them. In France, it was different. The bombed-out villages remained, the buildings mere shards against the glow of the setting sun. Bomb craters went unfilled, buildings left in ruins, village squares eerily silent, statues toppled and in pieces as if the French were saying—to themselves and the world: Look what was done to us! Do not forget! We will not forget!

Dorothy held up her end of conversation during the journey to Rouen, both to her friends and to herself, as she practiced her French. But as they got close to the city, a place Dorothy had dreamed about for years, she was, at first, without words.

What she saw, what they all saw . . . It's not as if the women hadn't seen what was left after air raids—Birmingham had endured more than its share of destruction. Some of the WACs, members of the first group of the 6888th to arrive in Europe, had barely dropped off their duffels, when a bomb found its target and shook the ground.

"It was like an earthquake," Fannie said, shaking her head from side to side. "I never felt anything like that." She had shuddered. "As if God stamped his foot."

The women had learned to accept the sight of collapsed homes, rubble piles of the leftovers, stone and wood, and the skeletal church spires silhouetted against a slate gray English sky. But they never got used to it.

That went double for Rouen, assaulted mercilessly by Germans, then occupied until late summer 1944, when they were finally driven out by Canadian troops. From one of the local women working at the postal directory, Dorothy learned that almost half of the old city was destroyed by air strikes and ground fighting— even the revered cathedral.

"Cathédrale Notre-Dame de Rouen," Dorothy said dreamily. She felt that her voice sounded its most elegant when she spoke in French. Her mates felt otherwise. The massive church was consecrated in 1063 in the presence of the man who would become William the Conqueror, but was left in pieces by Allied bombing to dislodge the German army in advance of D-Day. The city, too, was still in ruins, especially in an area stretching from the cathedral to the Seine, which was bombed and then burned unchecked for almost two days.

"The heart of Richard the Lionheart is there," Dorothy blurted out as she gazed out of the window, noting the damaged yet majestic spire of the cathedral rising in the distance. She couldn't help herself. These were tidbits too good to keep to oneself.

"Doro! No one cares! And who the heck is this Richard Lion guy anyway?" came a voice from two rows over.

"We don't care," murmured Hazel, who was sitting next to Dorothy.

"The great warrior king, called the 'Lionheart,'" Dorothy volunteered sheepishly. "The son of Henry II and . . ."

This time it was Leila who rolled her eyes.

"That's great, Dorothy, really," she said in a conciliatory tone. "But . . ."

"What I wanna know is, if his heart is here, where's the rest of him?" Hazel asked, a grin spreading across her face.

Riotous laughter sustained them until they arrived at the post and Dorothy made a note to herself to find out the answer.

*   *   *

"La caserne Tallandier à Petit-Quevilly."

Dorothy was one of the few women in the unit who could pronounce it properly. The new quarters consisted of a large brick building, formerly a cotton mill, and several outbuildings of good size. The complex was large enough to contain the entire battalion for work and housing. The pièce de résistance (Leila rolled her eyes when Dorothy said this) was the sturdily built wall that surrounded the compound. La caserne had served many purposes in its lifetime, from military fortress and barracks to mill. It had been built to last.

Leila thought it looked creepy. Hazel, unimpressed with most situations as usual, thought it looked decrepit. For Dorothy, enamored by any and everything français, it was romantic.

"I looked it up," she said in a dreamy voice.

"Of course you did," Hazel murmured, sotto voce.

"La caserne was used as a barracks by Napoleon's troops!" Dorothy said excitedly.

"What year was that?" Leila asked, studying the buildings with a frown on her face. "They look . . . old." She sniffed. "They smell old."

"They are old!" Dorothy confirmed with delight in her voice without realizing that Leila was not delighted to hear it. "They may even predate Bonaparte. Probably constructed in the 1790s or early 1800s."

"That figures," Hazel commented. "Built for soldiers. They don't look warm."

Leila's spirits sank lower.

"No, they don't," she agreed, remembering that the concept of "central heating" didn't extend reliably to their previous posting in Birmingham. Leila couldn't remember one day where she felt completely comfortable.

"Come on, girls, it's May!" Dorothy countered. "It'll warm up." Which was true. The calendar indicated that they were on the cusp of summer. But the barracks had the look of perpetual winter.

"It may be May," Hazel growled, "but from the looks of this place, I'll still be thawing out in July!"

They barely had time to drop their belongings. The city of Rouen had invited the 6888th to participate in festivities taking place that day in the city's center. After a flurry of disordered unpacking, cold water washing up, and voices raised in panic ("Where are my gloves?" "I can't find my shoes!") unit finally fell into formation behind their officers and CO, and made their way to the central city and the street of the clock to add their respects to Rouen's most esteemed woman and patron saint of France, Jeanne d'Arc.

Despite appearance and first impressions, la caserne Tallandier, the new home of the 6888th Post Directory Battalion, was neither as decrepit as Hazel thought nor as drafty as Leila feared. It *was* a vintage building but solid—built in the late 1700s, just before the *Ancien Régime* fell—but it had been renovated several times over the past 160 years, although it was not quite up to mid-twentieth century standards. As Leila suspected, its central heating was AWOL. But the buildings were dry (no leaky roofs) and spacious, and the entire unit fit within the substantial walls of the compound. A contingent of German POWs was assigned to make the old fort habitable.

In no time, the women settled into their quarters and into their work—sorting out the remaining mail and package stockpiles that been stored in France for the first part of the war. The officer and NCO clubs were set up, the kitchens supplied, and the work areas organized.

For this posting, Leila, who could type one hundred words per minute, was assigned to the admin office; Hazel's new assignment included coordinating the social clubs; and Dorothy returned her attention to the letter *V*—which dovetailed nicely with the residual celebrations that took place in Rouen and everywhere in Europe after VE Day on May 8. Or she would have done if she hadn't been ensconced for five days in a bed in the women's ward of l'Hôtel-Dieu, the local hospital, with a gastrointestinal complaint that sent her trotting back and forth to the latrines.

"Well, Dorothy. I have to hand it to you," Hazel teased, standing at Dorothy's bedside during a visit. "When you said that you wanted to visit the hospital where Flaubert was born, I had no idea that you would go to such lengths to get inside!"

Dorothy, whose midsection was sore, whose head still pounded, and whose complexion was an odd shade of puce mixed with lima bean green (she'd asked to look at her reflection in the mirror of Hazel's compact and was sorry that she did), was not amused.

Leila, who was standing on the other side of the bed, bit her lip.

"Have you gotten to see much of the hospital?" She suppressed a giggle.

Dorothy frowned.

"Only the toilet," she admitted with a sigh. But she'd made a vow to herself. The moment that she was feeling better and could manage two hours together without making a mad dash to the toilet, then, and only then, would she seek out *la maison du docteur*, the apartment where the great writer was born. But only, Dorothy thought, when she felt steady enough and didn't need the services of a *docteur* herself.

The day before she was released, she got her wish. One of the nurses had an uncle by marriage, long retired, who'd worked as a concierge for the hospital and a sometime caretaker for the building that housed the Flaubert apartment. It was a museum once, opened over twenty years ago, and now closed because of the war.

The nurse smiled.

Dorothy's breath caught in her throat.

"Do you think . . ." Dorothy repeated her question in French.

The nurse winked and picked up the lunch tray.

"Je pense . . . Oui. C'est possible. I think is possible that my uncle still has the keys," she said.

And he did.

Guy was eighty-six years old, had been a mason, a teamster, carpenter, and dog breeder—the massive Bouvier des Flandres were his pride and joy, and a velvet-eyed female named Blanche, her fur black as India ink, followed him everywhere. The "Jacques" of all trades, Guy had also been a shepherd and sailor in his younger days, as well as a ladies' man. Nurse Guilliame's aunt was wife number three. There was little about women or the old hospital and its illustrious former resident that he did not know.

The keys jiggled in Guy's hand as he touched the lock with a trembling hand. The door opened with a groan. Guy turned to Dorothy and bowed with as much gallantry as his body would allow.

"Entrez, mademoiselle," he said, his voice deep, gravelly, and seductive. His eyes were watery but steady, bright blue in the warm sunlight but with shades of slate and charcoal.

Un-huh, Dorothy said to herself, allowing her lips to form a slight smile. *This man was a Casanova when he was young.* She suppressed a giggle. Guy was really trying to make himself as attractive as possible. Not a small thing for man who looked to be at least as old as the building they were about to enter.

"Merci, monsieur," Dorothy replied.

"Avec plaisir," the old man said with a nod.

Dorothy wondered if her eyes were playing tricks on her because she thought that Uncle Guy just winked at her.

L'Hôtel-Dieu was old. It looked, smelled, and felt old. No, not old. Ancient. Built no one could remember exactly when, its buildings had been patched, repaired, and renovated over the centuries, but the hospital still felt like a relic. Over a century ago, its resident surgeon moved into an apartment on the grounds and it was there in 1821 that Gustave Flaubert was born. Dorothy stepped gingerly through the rooms, aware that it was like walking in a dollhouse. The spaces felt so small. Dusty and suffocating in the early summer heat—the museum had been closed for some time—the apartment seemed forlorn, the furniture (*Was it once used by the Flaubert family?* Dorothy wondered) was worn and shabby and the atmosphere of the years was palpable. She didn't feel the spark of inspiration that she'd thought she would, but she wasn't disappointed. Something about her favorite author was still here, floating in the molecules that made up the room. Dorothy was so lost in her thoughts that she didn't realize that Guy was talking.

"Pardon? Je suis désolée," she apologized, quickly processing what he had just asked.

The retired concierge smiled broadly. Dorothy smiled back. *The old flirt.*

"Non, merci," she replied. She couldn't have a drink with him this evening. She had already promised to go out with someone else.

* * *

Although they were doing the same work and using the same procedures, the new venue posed new and unexpected challenges. This was the first time that the women of the 6888th worked alongside French civilians, some of whom could speak a little English, some of whom could not. The language barrier created misunderstandings and Dorothy, one of the few WACs who was fluent in the language, acted as translator, sometimes as referee. It never ceased to amaze Dorothy how different the pronunciations were depending on the language. And how passionately each side—English or French—felt about whether a name was "George" or "Georges." And, not for the first time, the unit had to navigate resentment on the part of their local hosts because of the abundance of "luxuries," i.e., chocolate, cigarettes, and food. The attitudes dissipated somewhat once the locals realized that the 6888th's pantries included Spam, just as theirs did.

The women shared the mess with these POWs when they had work assignments at the old fort, although the two groups were domiciled apart. At Ft. Riley, they had interacted rarely and always with wariness. This time, the POWs, Germans, were part of the everyday landscape, although they were closely guarded and supervised by American soldiers. When they weren't on maintenance assignments at la caserne, they were marched away to points unknown for work detail. Fraternization was *verboten*.

But these men were polite and friendly, often waved, calling out, "Good morning, ladies," in heavily accented English. The bits of English that the POWs knew merged with the bits of German that the WACs knew, making the rare conversations they had rudimentary but practical. If a wall need to be painted or a chair repaired, one word of German plus an appropriate gesture did the trick. Most of the prisoners had been ordinary citizens before their military experience, carpenters, mechanics, bus drivers, etc. Like the women, they'd been civilians not soldiers. Under the watchful eyes of their guards, they did the work that needed doing to keep the old fort from crumbling and falling down on all their heads.

This was a contrast to the POWs that the women remembered

from their time at Ft. Riley. Dorothy still wished that she had thrown the soccer ball farther.

Hazel ran her hand across the top of an old peg-leg table that she had rescued from a rubbish heap on a backstreet in town. One of the legs was broken, the wood was splintered, and its surface was covered with filth. Despite that, Hazel saw it as the perfect addition to the general office, its area more spacious in la caserne than in Birmingham. A POW named "Ernst" had cleaned, sanded, and refurbished the table so well that its broken leg was unrecognizable from the unbroken ones.

"Good as new," Hazel commented, nodding with satisfaction. "One good thing about these Jerries. They haven't picked up any bad habits yet." She glanced at Dorothy who added, "Or bad words either."

SPAM PRIMAVERA

For the first few weeks at la caserne, the women of the 6888th ate like queens. The mess kitchen's pantry was well supplied with foodstuffs of all varieties, including fresh meat and dairy. The women ate almost too well. Specialist Glenda Jones, who was as handy with a needle and thread as she was wielding a pressing comb, managed a busy side hustle letting out seams and waistbands to accommodate expanding figures. One of the spec sergeants organized a calisthenics group to help work off the extra pounds that the women had gained. Major Adams was especially fond of fried chicken, and the mess hall staff complied with gusto, setting off amiable disagreements about whose chicken was best and whether the pieces should be dipped in egg wash, then flour before frying or flour alone. This tasty state of affairs came to a crashing end when a rudimentary inspection by the inspector general's office revealed that the 6888th had been categorized inaccurately as a "hospital unit," and therefore eligible for the more nutritious and fresh food supplies. The IG had assumed that a unit of eight hundred plus women could only be a contingent of nurses assigned to a hospital unit not a postal service. Once the classification was corrected, new orders were given to the quartermaster and the nature of the supply deliveries changed, much to the CO's chagrin. No more fresh chickens, vegetables, or dairy. Canned (or "tinned" as the Brits would say) everything, including meats along with powdered eggs, the taste and texture of which Dorothy couldn't stand. The mess hall staff did what they could, but even they were at their wits end when the complaints rolled in. Salt, pepper, and other seasonings were helpful but didn't solve the problem. The food was bland and unappetizing to look at. And although Major Adams understood better than anyone why the food supply complements had changed, she sorely missed her fried chicken, mashed potatoes, and gravy.

Rainey Barbour, who'd commandeered the mess kitchens at Ft. Riley and whose gravy was legendary, had exhausted the boundaries of her recipes. There was only so much a person could do with tinned pink-colored meat. One morning, after breakfast and before the lunch seating, Rainey stood on the back steps—she called it her "stoop"—and smoked one Chesterfield after another in frustration, blowing smoke rings. She stared off into space. The nicotine helped her think, sharpening her mind but not enough to come up with another casserole using Spam. With a sigh, she stubbed out the cigarette and felt around the pocket of her apron for another. To her disappointment, the pack was empty, but she had a chocolate bar so she unwrapped it and slid it into her mouth without even tasting it, thinking about a carton of cigarettes she had in her locker in the barracks, and that maybe she'd pop over and grab a pack . . . Oh yes, and she'd have to remember the chocolate bars she'd promised to bring to Cecile, one of the local women who helped out in the mess, in trade for a bottle of . . .

Abruptly, Rainey stood up straight and blinked. She'd been daydreaming, staring at the fortification that surrounded the barracks and the mess hall and other buildings, imagining the bucolic vistas beyond. The fort was situated at the edge of the city, where the houses were farther apart and there were gardens everywhere. Not far beyond this lay clumps of forests here and there, gently rolling hills, and fields where cattle and sheep grazed. Rainey inhaled sharply. Farms. Farms meant farmers. A farmer who had sheep or cattle probably kept chickens. Which meant eggs. And a farmer who had fields that weren't fallow might be growing fresh green beans, cabbages, carrots, or . . . Rainey turned on her heel and ran back into the kitchen, tearing off her apron as she sprinted.

"Lorraine, what's going on? Where you goin' so fast?" one of the mess hall workers called after her.

"To get some cigarettes!" Rainey yelled over her shoulder. To herself, she added, *And chocolates and chewing gum and Ivory soap!* A quick stop at the PX was required. Cecile had mentioned an uncle who lived close by, who was a *farmer*, and who was partial to American cigarettes. She hoped that he'd like Chesterfields. As Rainey ran, she wondered if he also liked gum and bar soap. And then . . . She was scheming as she ran. Rainey could drive, not well, but she could manage. She wondered if the CO would let her requisition a jeep. Then she had another thought. Cecile's uncle probably didn't speak English. But that didn't matter because Rainey knew someone who spoke French. She grinned as she headed over to the workroom and stood in the doorway, huffing a bit as she caught her breath, looking toward the workstation where the letter *V* was prominently displayed.

Dorothy's first foray into the countryside surrounding Rouen yielded an abundance of cabbages, beans, carrots, and eggs. The ones that followed yielded even more goodies, including bottles of the local red wine. Rainey and her mess hall staff took turns riding shotgun on these excursions and even Dorothy drove a few times, to the delight of the French farmers. They teased her because, being barely five feet tall, she had to sit on a cushion and could barely reach the pedals. The German POWs reciprocated with equal hilarity when they saw the jeep bouncing along with Dorothy in the driver's seat, hollering after her and calling her *"die kleine Frau"* which meant "a little woman." With the CO's approval, Dorothy now had two work assignments: redirecting the mail (she was still amazed at how many *V*s there were) and serving as chief translator-driver in the late afternoons and evenings. Chickens were still difficult to come by, but the abundance of fresh vegetables, mushrooms, and eggs allowed Rainey, Edna, and the mess hall kitchen staff to create tastier and more colorful meals, including one that became a battalion specialty that even the locals enjoyed—a concoction of sautéed vegetables, olive oil, salt, pepper, and grated local cheese mixed with cubed Spam served atop a mound of spaghetti. They called it "Spam primavera." The tech specialist's calisthenics group, which had been disbanded due to lack of interest, came together again.

By late summer, Dorothy's second job was wearing her out. The amount of *V* mail that needed handling was beginning to diminish—many of the soldiers had been mustered out or assigned to the Pacific theater. The postal unit was winding down, and there was talk that some of the women would be transferred to Paris before their return to the States. But the barter arrangement with the local community had yielded such bounty that Dorothy was as busy as ever and, often, didn't return from her country travels until early evening. Sometimes she would eat and then go out with Leila and Hazel to their favorite local watering hole, just off the street of the clock. Other evenings, she'd grab a plate from the mess hall and fall into bed, exhausted.

One night the women returned late from the countryside and Dorothy, too tired to eat, decided to go to bed early. She crossed the courtyard from the motor pool toward the barracks near the rear of the compound. It was still light, but dusk was falling. The courtyard wasn't deserted, but it was quiet for a change—many of the women spent their evenings in town or in the rec area playing cards or Ping-Pong. It was the end of July, but the weather felt like home to Dorothy, like a late summer day in Georgia, sultry and still. A movement caught her eye and she turned her head to speak. At the far edge of the yard, she saw a figure, but he—she assumed that it was a "he" because of height—was in a shadow created by the perimeter pole lights and the courtyard itself was dim, so she couldn't see well enough to recognize a face or even a uniform. If she hadn't been so tired, she might have wondered more; the POWs were already locked in for the night and there weren't any other men on the post. Even the MPs were women. Dorothy raised her hand in greeting but the figure slipped from view. Dorothy shrugged her shoulders and continued walking toward the lights in the window of the barracks. She heard a rustling sound behind her and looked over her shoulder. But there was no one there. A light breeze brushed her cheek with cool fingers.

Yawning, Dorothy opened the door; it creaked and stuck, and she thought to remind herself in the morning to ask the corporal who supervised the POWs if one of the men could see to the door. She dragged herself in, thinking about the warm shower that she would take, the softness of her pillow (thank you, Aunt Denie, for packing bed linens) and made a bet with herself as to how many times she'd have to tell the girls to lower their voices because she was trying to sleep. She stopped short. The barracks was practically silent even though it was nearly full. Women gathered in small clumps here and there. Some of them sat on their beds, dabbing their eyes. Others wept openly, leaning against each other for support. The atmosphere was heavy and warm.

An authorized social engagement at a nearby military post. Three WACs, Mary Bankston, Mary Barlow, Delores Browne. A traffic accident. The jeep overturned. The two Marys were dead. Delores was nearly so. Five days later, she died too.

The women were distraught. It was inconceivable. The Six Triple Eight was not a combat unit, even their MPs were unarmed. They weren't accustomed to casualties or deaths. Not in this way, not by a road accident that could happen anywhere, here or in the States. They sorted mail. They weren't and had never been in harm's way. There was no reason to expect that all eight hundred fifty-five women would not return safely to the United States once the war was over. And yet.

In the following week, Dorothy remembered something that her mother, Eva, had told her about when Grandmother Harriet died decades ago, long before Dorothy was born. Harriet's sisters had come en masse—there were four of them—and taken care of the laying out. It was 1907. There was no one else to do it. "Birth and death," Eva had said. "They're women's work."

There were no provisions for funerals in the army regulations either, not for WACs, no funds allocated for mortuary services or caskets. No mechanism to do or pay for what had to be done. So the women of the 6888th did it themselves. They took up a collection to pay for the wood and the POWs made the caskets. The women arranged for the services. Within the unit, there were WACs who had worked in mortuaries and funeral homes. They prepared the bodies. Two services were held in the hospital chapels, one Protestant and one Catholic. And, finally, after tearful salutes, Private First Class Mary Bankston, Private First Class Mary Barlow, and Sergeant Delores Browne were buried at the American military cemetery in Normandy at Colleville-sur-Mer. Women's work.

Verboten

am telling you that it was the ghost." Edna, who always sounded as if she was sure about everything, sounded doubly sure about this. "No question about it."

"Eddie, really? Ghosts? I don't believe in ghosts." This from Hazel, who was as sure that ghosts were nonsense as Edna was that they were real.

Dorothy rolled her eyes. Now she was sorry that she'd mentioned her encounter with whatever "it" was several weeks before.

"A ghost," she said. "What ghost? I've never heard about any ghosts around this place."

"Then you haven't been listening," Edna snapped. "You and your en français! Of course there are ghosts! This place is old as Jesus's socks."

Leila snorted.

"Our Lord wore sandals, Eddie, so no socks," someone shouted.

"I'm getting' outa here," came a voice from the other side of the room. "Y'all bout to get us struck by lightning talking about Jesus and his socks!"

"Too much French country air," another woman chirped.

"Too much French country *wine*," Hazel added.

Dorothy swatted at her.

Laughter followed this remark, but Edna would not be moved.

"Listen up here," Edna countered, the twangy tones of Tennessee seasoning her voice. "This place has seen *some* times past. The French Revolution, Napoleon's boys stayed here, it was a cotton mill, it's got atmosphere, you can feel it."

That was true. There was an aura about the old fort.

Dorothy sighed. She had seen something, a shadow maybe, but a ghost?

Edna gave her a side-eye.

"Don't get cute with me, Dorothy. You said you felt a chill."

"Yes, well, all right. I did."

"Uh-huh," Edna said, nodding with satisfaction.

"I give. So what ghost are we talking about, Eddie? Does he . . . it have a name?"

Edna held up one finger and began to count.

"There's more than one?" Dorothy asked, now regretting that she'd asked.

"There was a witch burned at the stake in the courtyard . . ."

"No, it was a heretic priest, burned during the Inquisition!" one woman interjected.

"The Inquisition was in Spain, Genny," another woman said.

"Spain, France, whatever. They're next to each other!"

"Well, I heard that one of the Napoleonic soldiers was executed . . ."

"No, it was a Prussian soldier and he was . . ."

"German sniper! In the Great War, the French caught him on a hill outside the city . . ."

"No, no, you've got it all wrong!" one of the sergeants shouted. "It was a German *pilot*! His plane went down, the French pulled him out and executed him. He's buried here on the grounds. Somewhere . . ."

"In the courtyard!"

"Wait. What's the difference between German and Prussian? Because I'm sure that . . ."

By this time, Dorothy, Hazel, Leila, and even Edna had a case of the giggles.

"Mercy!" Dorothy commented. "All these ghosts!"

"Don't worry about it, he won't hurt you."

This time, Dorothy resisted rolling her eyes in disbelief.

"Which ghost are we talking about, Eddie? And how would you know that? Did he tell you personally?"

Edna shrugged.

"I've got a feel for this sort of thing, like my momma. Like her momma and on back. We feel the spirits. This one? He's just one lonely soul looking for a place to be. Lost. Not gonna hurt ya. Just wants to be . . . just wants to be noticed. To be recognized."

"It'd be nice if he could be recognized somewhere else!" Leila said, rubbing her arms as if she was chilled. "Does it have to be here?"

"Holy water. That'll do the trick," Mobile, Alabama–born Anita commented. "I'll ask Father Grimeau after Mass."

Dorothy and Leila locked eyes and both grinned. Dorothy thought about Big Dad's Ebenezer Baptist, which didn't hold with images, incense, or holy water, but unlike her grandfather, she was willing to keep an open mind. If the sprinkling dissipated the eerie chill of la caserne's courtyard, who was she to object?

* * *

A few weeks later, Dorothy and Rainey headed back to post from another successful round of farm visits, the jeep loaded with fresh, colorful produce. Rainey spent most of the return trip designing recipes in her head to make the most of the midsummer bounty. Dorothy drove feeling like a queen on a throne sitting atop her pillow. But as they rounded a turn on the homestretch, the vehicle jerked and dropped into a pothole that looked like what was left of a small crater with such ferocity that one of the bushels overturned and Dorothy was nearly knocked off her perch in the driver's seat. Dorothy pulled over to the side of the road. She and Rainey looked at each other for a moment, then got out of the jeep to survey the damage. They shared the same thought. The motor accident that killed their sister WACs was fresh in their minds. Dorothy shivered. Rainey's face was pale.

"What do you think?" she asked, a frown expanding across her face as she looked at the wheel.

Dorothy exhaled loudly. She looked down the road toward

Rouen. It wound sharply to the left, then disappeared around a bend. There was a slight hill there as the road entered a small copse of trees. In the distance, Dorothy could see the spire of the Notre Dame Cathedral of Rouen. She bit her lip, then shrugged.

"It's not far. Let's give it a try."

They were only a few miles from the post. The rim was cracked, but it was so grimy that it was hard to tell if it was about to come to pieces or not. Dorothy debated with herself with her fingers crossed. Was the rim damaged so badly that it wouldn't hold together for a bit longer? She scrambled back into the seat, started up the engine, and said a prayer. Then she depressed the clutch. The engine turned over, nothing wrong with it, and the jeep rolled forward slowly but continuously and limped into la caserne's makeshift garage. They were immediately surrounded by the mechanics on duty, including the German POWs who worked there. With fanfare, the men helped Dorothy and Rainey out of the vehicle, then unloaded the produce. After dispatching a couple of the men to take the food to the mess hall, the officer in charge and the mechanics stood in a circle studying the damaged rim with the solemnity of surgeons consulting on a complicated medical case. They clucked and harrumphed, clearing their throats as they batted comments back and forth in English, German, and a hybrid of English-German-French. Dorothy, whose knowledge of the German language was rudimentary at best, occasionally caught the words "die kleine Frau," so she knew that the men were also talking about her.

The corporal who supervised the garage crew and spoke fluent German thanks to his Munich-born mother explained to the women that the diagnosis was as they thought: the wheel rim was bent and cracked but not critically so. The mechanics were confident that it could be fixed "tout de suite." He also told Dorothy, smiling, that the men held the "Little Woman" in high regard, saying that none of the other WACs could have handled the damaged jeep as well as she had.

As they walked back to the barracks, they passed the men who'd carried the produce to the mess hall. The men said, "Guten Tag," and removed their caps as they passed by, and one of them winked at Dorothy.

Rainey chuckled.

"I don't know if a wink in German means the same as a wink in American but I can tell you this. *That* wink was strictly verboten."

"As long as a hot shower isn't verboten, I don't care," Dorothy said as she imagined the pleasure of a warm waterfall descending from the showerhead, rinsing away the grit and dust and the barnyard odor that had attached themselves to her skin. A voice intruded on her daydream as she gathered up her shower things.

"Thom! You have a visitor!"

Dorothy groaned.

"Tell him to go away. I don't know anyone in Rouen. I don't know anyone in France. All I want is to be left alone under the showerhead. Thank you very much."

The woman laughed.

"Too bad for you then. This one says that he's your cousin."

Laughter filled the barracks.

"What?" the sergeant barked out, joining in the fun. "Thom, how many cousins do you have?"

"Not as many as you do, Sergeant!" she countered. The sergeant and the other women howled with laughter. Over the past couple of months, the women of the 6888th had had many unexpected visitors—all male—and the majority of these introduced themselves as "old family friends" or "cousins."

Almost from the first week that the unit took up quarters in la caserne, the busy yet organized atmosphere of the 6888th changed overnight to a state of chaos as soldiers released from active duty on the eastern front were being mustered out, reassigned, or given leave. Many of them made their way to Rouen, where they had heard there was a large contingent of female military personnel, specifically the postal directory battalion. Rouen quickly became the destination of choice for the men even if they didn't have an official reason to be there. Considering that these were soldiers who had not seen an American woman—Black or white—since 1942, Major Adams was at her wit's end. There was still postal work to be done, her women needed to feel secure in their posting, and worryingly, the CO did not have a large number of MPs at her disposal. She had thanked her lucky stars for the fortress-style layout of la caserne and for its prominent and substantially built gates, especially after she was told that there were 31 male officers for every female officer and 725 enlisted men for every enlisted woman. But at first, Adams misconstrued the level of urgency.

"Seven hundred twenty-five enlisted men?" she'd asked the officer, thinking to herself, *That's probably right.* "In the ETO, you mean."

The sergeant's expression was incredulous. She raised an eyebrow.

"No, ma'am. Outside our gates."

The CO's eyes widened as she did the math. Seven hundred twenty-five men for every woman? Just outside their gates?

It had taken quick thinking to manage what could have become a disaster. The major struggled to coordinate visits and contact between the service personnel while maintaining the cohesiveness of the all-female environment. Everyone appreciated the opportunity to relax and socialize and the women enjoyed spending time with their male counterparts. At one point there was a mob of men outside the gates clamoring to be let it, to "say hello" to this cousin or that sister or sweetheart. For the most part, although the men were vocal—"loud" was Dorothy's word for them—they behaved. But for the few who did not, the CO had concerns. The MPs assigned to the 6888th were all women and unarmed. Strangely, the army had not seen fit to guard its all-female battalion to that level, and when the CO formally made the request for firearms and training, she was turned down. Creative thinking solved the problem. A British soldier, an acquaintance of Major Adams who'd participated in the Battle of the Bulge and was still in France, offered to teach classes in jujitsu. It didn't take long for the unit to recognize the value of martial arts, especially when a petite PFC deftly took down a six-foot-tall male soldier without breaking a fingernail.

It didn't take long for the novelty to wear off. Dressing up from time to time was fine. Being perfectly turned out, hair, nails, and makeup all the time became a chore. Hair appointments still needed to be made. Undies still had to be washed and hung to dry. The enthusiastic smiles began to wane. A contingent of noncoms delivered a request to Major Adams.

"Get rid of the men!"

From that point forward a "No men on Monday" policy was put in place. And only men who had the proper name of the woman that they wanted to see were allowed on post; "cousins" and "old family friends" were subject to much closer scrutiny.

Dorothy shook her head and marched toward the showers.

"No cousins today, thank you!!"

"Doro!"

The noncom laughed too but stayed on point.

"Dorothy, he says that your mother and his mother are sisters. His mother's name is . . . Alvin?" The noncom's expression shifted. Now *she* wondered if maybe this soldier wasn't on the level. What woman would have a name like Alvin?

But Dorothy stopped and looked over her shoulder.

"Alvin."

The noncom nodded.

"Then he is my cousin," Dorothy said, staring at the woman. "He's Aunt Alvin's boy."

COUSIN DOROTHY

He was about two years old the first time Dorothy and her sisters met him. Aunt Alvin was their mother's youngest sister who used her middle name "Clara" in the wider world. But the family still called her "Alvin." It was summer and Eva had brought her girls, Hattie, Rosa, and Dorothy, to Eatonton to visit with Big Dad. Aunt Alvin had come down on the train from Ohio with her little one. The toddler, Harold was his name, was chubby and drooled a lot (Aunt Alvin said that he was teething), and he walked like a little bear, lumbering from side to side on his short fat legs. Aunt Alvin thought he was the cutest thing. Even Dorothy's mother, Eva, was charmed by him, and that was saying something. Eva was not fond of babies despite having had five children. Big Dad took the little boy in hand and walked him around the garden, murmuring stories to him and stopping once or twice to pick him up when he'd fallen into the tomatoes or green bean vines. Dorothy and her sisters were not impressed with the little boy at all and after saying a polite hello to their aunt, they made a hasty exit to a remote area of Big Dad's sprawling yard to continue their more grown-up games. Hattie was thirteen, Rose was twelve, and Dorothy was nine.

The young man standing in front of her in the hall outside the recreation area nervously working his hat in his large hands did not look at all like the little terror that Dorothy remembered. He was taller than she was—well, everyone was taller than Dorothy—muscular and handsome with a long slender face, dark expressive brows, and neatly cropped hair that complemented his pecan-colored complexion. He nodded and said, "Hello," speaking slowly, his words sounding clipped and flat compared to the rounded soft tones of Georgia that had characterized Aunt Alvin's voice despite living over twenty years in the Midwest. Harold had grown up in Ohio; his parents left the South before he was born and Uncle Richard worked on the Pennsylvania Railroad. He was Midwestern, unlike Dorothy, who, despite the time she'd spent in Cleveland with her mother, still had Georgia in her bones. He held out his hand, smiling, his teeth white and perfect. Dorothy did the math. He was about twenty, twenty-two at most. Suddenly, she felt like an old woman.

"Cousin Dorothy, I hope you don't mind that I dropped in like this, unannounced," he said. "I'm going home. Heard that you women . . . that your unit was here. Mother said that you were part of it." He looked around at the activity in the recreation room—turned–NCO club. "This is some place!"

Dorothy laughed and hugged him.

"So when did you hear from Aunt Alvin?"

"Not too long ago," Harold answered. "I got five letters all at once! Her first letter was over a year old! But I guess it took you all some time to get caught up."

That's an understatement.

Dorothy smiled, thinking of the many hours she and her sister WACs had spent in the musty boys' school gymnasium squinting to read the handwriting on the change-of-address cards, especially in the evenings when the blackout curtains covered the windows. It felt good knowing that her own family had benefited from their efforts. She gestured toward a table and chairs.

"Would you like something to drink?"

"Yes, ma'am," Harold said politely. Then, blushing, he said, "Sorry. Yes, please."

Dorothy grinned.

"Lemonade, Coca-Cola? Or something stronger?"

Now it was Harold's turn to grin.

"Lemonade is fine, Cousin Dorothy. Mother would not approve of me drinking anything stronger," he said, laughter in his voice.

But we both know that you do, and so do I! Dorothy said to herself. Aunt Alvin was strictly teetotal.

Soon, they were sipping the tart, cold lemonade, progressing quickly from their awkward greetings to conversation about family—their mothers in particular—Big Dad, and what was going on next in Harold's life. He talked animatedly about a young woman he'd met who lived in New Jersey. As the afternoon progressed, there'd been a shift change and now the makeshift NCO club was buzzing with voices in animated conversation and laughter. The sound of cards slapped down on tabletops in victory and ice tinkling against glass competed with the click-clack of Ping-Pong balls against paddle and table to complement the upbeat music playing in the background.

"What unit are you with?" Dorothy asked. She'd met so many young men lately coming from all over Europe, many of them detaching from Poland, eastern Germany, Holland, Belgium, and France. The stories about their experiences were riveting, and she was eager to hear about Harold's war. She hadn't even known that he was in the service, although she wasn't surprised. Many men of her acquaintance, including her brothers, had enlisted.

Harold was quiet for a moment, took another sip of his drink. His expression was somber.

"The 761st," he said in a voice so low that she barely heard it.

Oh. She felt a twinge in her stomach. The Battle of the Bulge. He'd been with Patton in the east. Dorothy had heard devastating stories about the action from returning soldiers passing through Rouen. She didn't say anything because there wasn't anything to say. Her cousin was here now, all in one piece, sitting in front of her and sipping lemonade. He had likely seen the worst of it, had in all probability watched as his buddies were shot and died. She noticed now that the animation and smile had left Harold's face and his eyes were blank, staring inward at a horror that she could not imagine. His hands, which just a moment ago were resting palms down on the table, had curled themselves into fists. The stories. So much devastation and death. The 333rd, an all Negro unit, had almost been wiped out. The 761st, a tank battalion, had been hit hard. But it would be no comfort to Harold to congratulate him that he had survived. For him, that would not be a milestone to celebrate. She wondered how long it would be before his memories of the experience would fade enough to allow him to unclench his hands. The image of those hands was now fused into her memory. Every soldier's war, whether they'd seen combat or not, would be a part of their life as long as they lived. In boot camp, the sergeants had said, "Once in the army, always in the army," and Dorothy believed it. The impact of the Blitzkrieg, Dunkirk, D-Day, dogfights, the film footage of the liberation of Auschwitz-Birkenau in January, and the German retreat after the Battle of the Bulge was imprinted now and embedded in her psyche even though she had not been physically present. They were a part of her now. It would be some time before Dorothy saw the film of the atomic bomb mushroom clouds that marked the destruction of Hiroshima and Nagasaki in August. But those images would become a part of her too.

On September 5, 1945, the Japanese surrendered and the second war of wars was over. The women of the 6888th celebrated with the people of Rouen in the city center and in the bistros and clubs in the streets surrounding the street of the clock. Major Adams received orders to split the unit in two, sending one contingent to Paris and leaving the other behind in Rouen to complete the work there. And as in the poem "Abou Ben Adhem," Dorothy was not called first or at all. She remained on assignment at la caserne in Rouen. But she did go to Paris.

S'IL VOUS PLAÎT

Fall 1945
Paris, France

Dorothy hitched a ride with a quartet of clerks on reassignment to the 6888th's Paris posting and bunked with the other enlisted women in the Hotel Bohy Lafayette located in Montmartre near Le Sacré-Coeur. Once she stepped out of the truck and onto the Parisian street, she was in heaven and it wasn't just because she'd felt as if she'd nearly died, seeing her life pass before her eyes on the roads out of Rouen. The French were notoriously fast and mercurial drivers and the jeep made several hard stops on its journey to Paris. All was forgotten once she arrived. It didn't matter that she wasn't posted here and would have to sleep on the floor. She didn't care that she only had the weekends to explore. It didn't matter that it was raining. The only thing that mattered was that she was in Paris. That she could walk up the hill and see the glorious basilica and its magnificent dome that gleamed white even on a cloudy day. That she could catch a bus and arrive in front of le Louvre. And that she wasn't far from one of the many bridges that spanned la Seine. She walked across to the Left Bank.

The streets were teeming with life, Parisian and military. Most everyone was young, many were in uniform, and all were in high spirits. Dorothy and her friends explored the old city without a fixed destination, happily getting lost in this or that arrondissement, taking the metro and missing the proper stop and eating too much. As the weeks passed, they copied Parisian street fashion, piling their hair into pompadours and walking the sidewalks precariously balanced on the newest French craze: platform heeled shoes. At barely five feet tall, Dorothy was an instant fan, although she wrenched her ankle when a heel caught in the cobblestones.

Every moment of leave that Dorothy had was spent in Paris. She explored and window-shopped during the day and spent time in the clubs at night, laughing and drinking with the jubilant Allied soldiers stationed in the city. The Brits were funny, generous, and polite. The French were more reserved but immediately warmed to Dorothy because she could speak their language. The Dutch soldiers were a bit stern but friendly in their own way. And the "Yanks," as the Brits called them, were, well, it was complicated.

In many of the clubs, the soldiers mixed with no regard to uniform, country of origin, or color. The common threads were that they'd beat the Nazis, wanted to celebrate, and loved the music, whatever it was. Occasionally, the women would notice a man in an American uniform studying them with an expression that could only be described as disdain, but it didn't happen often and everyone was having such a good time that the sour faces were easily overlooked. What was lovely, however, was the opportunity to socialize with the Negro soldiers returning from all points of the front. Hazel spent a lot of time with one of the Negro airmen, Leila was being charmed by a persistent but charming British military chaplain, and Dorothy was surrounded by a RAF intelligence officer, a French *capitaine*, and a Negro sergeant and basked in the attention. Ralph invited Dorothy to visit his family in the Yorkshire countryside; she discussed the short stories of Colette with Yves and jazz with Don, who was from Philadelphia.

"What d'you think, Miss Dorothy?" Don's grin had wattage that would light up a room. "How about you and I say good night to these gentlemen here and go for a more . . . private celebration."

Dorothy's antenna went up. She glanced over at the table where Leila and Hazel were sitting. She was enjoying her evening and especially the attention from the handsome officers and their spirited conversation. She wasn't looking for anything serious and she certainly wasn't planning to visit the hotel room of a man that she'd just met.

"*Non!*" Yves exclaimed. "You can't leave now! We just getting the beginning!" He grinned, proud of his attempt at American English.

The Brit agreed, holding his glass aloft.

"Whatever he said, I agree! Amen to that!" he said. "Another toast to Dorothy! Hear, hear!"

"*Santé!*"

"To Dorothy!"

Don leaned close to Dorothy and whispered, "Let's get outa here, girl. I've got a room at the Lilianne up the street where you and I can . . . entertain each other without these clowns." The sergeant's voice was low and seductive. Dorothy felt a shiver of desire down her spine. She could imagine having a pleasant experience with Sergeant Don Rodgers. But not now, not this evening. Not ever, really, if she was honest. Her thoughts were elsewhere. She touched glasses with the other two men and laughed.

"*Santé!*"

"Not tonight, Don," she murmured. "I just want to sit back, relax, and enjoy the music."

"I got some music you'd enjoy, baby," the sergeant responded, moving closer.

For a moment Dorothy relaxed. Don's voice was smooth and warm like velvet and . . . Dorothy flinched. *Wait a minute.* Don had placed his palm on her thigh and was lightly stroking the bare skin above her stocking with his fingertips. How dare he? She jerked her leg away from his probing hand and gave him a sharp glance of disapproval to boot. But Sergeant Rodgers was no quitter. He replaced his palm and tightened his grip on Dorothy's thigh.

Her inclination was to give the man an elbow, stand up, kick her chair away, and yell, "Oh, hell no!" while giving him a kick as well. But, not wanting to make a scene (although he deserved it), she did none of these, engaged as she was in conversation with Ralph and Yves. They laughed at the remark Dorothy made. Then she took another sip of champagne and, still smiling, leaned in close to Don. His eyes lit up with anticipation.

"If you don't take your hand off my thigh," she murmured in a voice dripping with acid and honey, "I'll grind my heel into the toe of your shoe, give you a jab in the gut, and throw this lovely drink in your face, which would be a real shame and a waste of good champagne." She winked at him then growled, "I'm gonna count to two."

The sergeant's bedroom eyes and seductive grin melted away and a mask of indignant and righteous anger took its place. He slammed his drink down on the table, nearly knocking the Brit's whiskey over, and stood up, his chair toppling over from the violence of his action.

Dorothy stood up too in a fury. She was two feet away from being nose to nose with the sergeant, although he towered over her.

"Here now!" Ralph bellowed.

"*Merde!*" Yves exclaimed.

"Siddity stuck-up bitch!" Don said, loudly. "You think you all that 'cause you went to college. I can get ten women right now." He snapped his fingers. "I don't need your Black ass anyway. I can get what I want from the white girls."

"Then I wonder why you're bothering me!" Dorothy bellowed, her voice and her temper rising with every word. *He has some nerve!* "Obviously I'm not your type at all!"

"Damn right about that!" Don bellowed. He stormed off, awakening the irritation of Ralph and Yves, who were outraged at the insult, and the curiosity of Dorothy's friends, who were sitting at the next table. The women ran over to where Dorothy had been sitting.

"Doro? What the heck is going on?" Hazel asked.

"You all right?" Leila and Rainey asked in a duet.

The RAF officer and the capitaine started talking simultaneously in English and French, but Hazel only had ears for Dorothy.

"What was that all about?" Hazel murmured.

Dorothy shrugged with a nonchalance that she did not feel.

"Nothing." She looked over at the door where Sergeant Rodgers had just exited.

"Dorothy, it doesn't look like nothing," Hazel said, also looking toward the door where the man had exited.

Dorothy shrugged. "Lovers' quarrel."

Leila snorted.

"Lovers' quarrel my behind," she countered. "Really, Doro?"

Dorothy shrugged and raised her champagne.

"Okay. Mistaken identity. He had me confused with someone who wanted his grubby palm on their thigh!"

A second glass of champagne and a half hour of laughter and conversation cooled Dorothy's temper and lifted her spirits. The pilot and the capitaine pulled tables together so that Dorothy's friends could join them, and the party continued as if there had never been an interruption, as if Sergeant Rodgers had never been there.

Except. Dorothy sipped her champagne.

The only reason she had chatted with Don Rodgers in the first place and flirted with him was because he reminded her of someone, only at the time she'd met the sergeant—at a picnic in the Tuileries—she couldn't remember who it was. Now, his boorish behavior excavated the name: Jimmy Wells, Staff Sergeant James W. Wells, an Ohio native she'd met in Rouen at a festival on the street of the clock. He was passing through, on his way to Le Havre and home. They shared a few drinks, a friendly conversation, and a chaste hug. They had exchanged addresses. He was tall and lean like Rodgers with a broad smile and dark eyes. But the similarities ended there. His voice was low and soft, and although the way he looked at Dorothy was anything but chaste (Dorothy could feel the warmth down her spine), Jimmy had called her "Ma'am," held her arm gently as they crossed the street, and never touched her thigh.

"I would like to hear from you sometime," he said. "When you come home. To know how you're getting on."

Dorothy couldn't imagine Sergeant Rodgers giving two hoots how she was "getting on." She had placed the slip of paper with Jimmy's address on it into her pocket notebook. She hoped that it was still there.

*   *   *

Rouen was seventy miles from Paris, give or take. It took the cumbersome military trucks two and a half to three hours to make the trip, taking into consideration French drivers and the city traffic. Dorothy got lucky with her ride back to la caserne, hitching another ride with a group of military nurses. The women chattered among themselves, laughing and telling stories as they passed through French countryside, the trees now changing colors from green to gold, orange, and sienna. Fortunate enough to nab a seat by the window, Dorothy rested her forehead against the cool glass and closed her eyes, reliving the past few days she'd spent in the city that she'd dreamed about all of her life. The bohemian feel of Montmartre and the majesty of Le Sacré-Coeur. The beautiful Seine and its bridges. She'd managed to slip away to the Île de la Cité just as the bells rang for noon mass at Notre Dame. And she'd lit a candle in the nave. She'd thought to join some of the girls and their new male friends for an October picnic of bread, cheese, and wine in front of the Eiffel Tower but had decided against it in favor of a visit to Pére Lachaise Cemetery to pay respects to her muses, Chopin, Balzac, and of course, the divine Oscar Wilde. But Dorothy hadn't missed anything by saying "*non.*" Everywhere she went she could see the tower. Just the thought of it made her smile.

She had saved the best for last. Le Louvre had reopened and, while it was not yet back to its prewar condition, the curators and museum workers were busy, up to their knees in packing crates and sawdust as they began the arduous task of repopulating the old museum with its priceless art. The keepers of le Louvre had tried to anticipate the worst just before Paris fell and stripped the museum of its treasures, hiding them as creatively as they could so that the Nazis would not find them. Now, they were being restored to their rightful place and Dorothy and her friends delighted at the sight of Renoirs and da Vincis being hung on the old walls.

"I didn't realize that she was so . . . small," Leila said, turning her head to the side as she studied the da Vinci portrait of a wealthy Florentine woman.

"Something about that smile though," Dorothy commented. "Hmmm, I wonder. What is she smiling about?"

Hazel giggled.

"Might have somethin' to do with what she was doin' before she posed for that painting!"

They started their afternoon in the Grand Gallery, then wandered through the museum until their feet hurt. Their last stop would be Dorothy's favorite on the Daru Staircase, where the Greek statue of the goddess Nike reigned, its ivory marble glowing in the fall sunlight. Dorothy stopped in her tracks. The statue was almost twenty feet tall and damaged—the head and arms were missing— but the imagination filled in the images of what was missing and the wings spreading out from the goddess's shoulder blades evoked power, resilience, and beauty. It was over two thousand years old, a gift from the people of Rhodes to Samothrace as an offering to the gods.

Dorothy was spellbound. She thought that this was the most beautiful piece of art she'd ever seen. The wings, especially the wings. *Which are a symbol*, she thought. *A symbol of freedom, a symbol of expanding possibilities.*

"We'll come back here, you know." Dorothy looked over her shoulder where Hazel stood, her eyes wide as she took in the beauty of the marble winged goddess. "Let's make a promise be- tween ourselves, to come back here. Maybe not every year . . ."

"Probably not every year!" Leila echoed, chuckling.

"Every three years, maybe," Hazel mused. "Even when we're little old ladies. Well. Maybe one little old lady. Dorothy! Leila and I will just be old ladies!"

"Promise," Leila said in a solemn voice. "To see this thing of beauty. And to remember what we've been through, our adven- tures."

"Agreed," Hazel said, nodding.

"Yes," Dorothy added, tears filling her eyes.

Leila looked over at Hazel and winked.

"En français s'il vous plaît," she said. Her pronunciation was atrocious and Dorothy couldn't resist laughing.

"Oui," she said.

WINGED VICTORY

December 1945
Rouen, Le Havre, and New York

They might not have returned as planned. In addition to several hundred members of the Six Triple Eight, a contingent of nurses were also on board. The ship's captain, following protocol, coordinated the sailing and activities with the highest-ranking WAC officer on board, Major Adams. For the white nurses, that was a difficulty, and the difficulty grew into a problem and nearly a fracas as the nurses vocally expressed their refusal to take orders from a Negro. The ship captain, operating under his own orders and procedures, was more concerned about leaving port on time and safely crossing the Atlantic than he was about the out-of-joint noses of the nurses. The ultimatum was simple: follow the command of Major Adams or leave the ship and do it quickly so that the schedule could be met. The nurses stayed on board.

It was a rough crossing. That should have been expected. Anyone who knew anything about the Atlantic, even people who'd never been to sea, knew that crossing the Atlantic in winter, and December was definitely winter, knew that the ocean was mercurial. The *George Washington*, which was in its prewar life a Germany luxury yacht, was now a troop transport and the "luxury" moniker of its former sailings was only a memory. The ship rolled and tossed its way across the Atlantic, finally docking in New York and discharging its queasy and disgruntled military passengers, Dorothy included.

She was sent to Ft. Bragg for two weeks, mustered out of the army, and sent home—Cleveland this time—to ponder the next step in her life. It turned out to be more difficult than she imagined because she had been places and done things that no one like her had done before. Going back to third grade teaching or managing a college reading room was unthinkable. Living out the rest of her life in Cleveland or Atlanta or anywhere without the possibility of using the passport now issued in her name was ridiculous. Dorothy, Leila, Hazel, and some of their other WAC sisters had agreed to meet every other year if possible—in the States or in Europe. As Edna joked, "You can't keep 'em down on the plantation after they've seen Paree!"

And Edna was right. Dorothy wouldn't stay in Cleveland long. Her mind twirled with ideas and possibilities. She wrote them down in a little clothbound notebook that she'd bought off a street vendor in the Marais in Paris. And she put the little book into a small wooden box that she kept in the nightstand next to her bed. She closed the lid and her hand lingered for a moment on the smooth flat surface. The carver had hand-painted a bucolic nineteenth century scene of a house beside a stream with ducks and people. The image was fuzzy, deliberately so, Dorothy thought, but it was pleasant and dreamy, designed to make you smile. And she did smile, remembering her last days at la caserne in Rouen.

Everyone was busy, rushing here and there, making arrangements, sending boxes and furniture to the quartermaster's warehouse, packing up this, giving away that, saying goodbye. It was strange seeing the old fort looking almost as it had when they'd first arrived, the courtyard and buildings empty but prepared, clean like a child eagerly waiting for company who would bring gifts of industry, furniture, food, cigarette smoke, and laughter. The stone walls, ancient and worn, now had no adornments, and the flagstones and wooden floors had been scrubbed. As the women finished their work, their conversations echoed around the vacant rooms, sounding as if they were ghosts too, remnants from Napoleon's day taking the opportunity to finally make themselves heard. La caserne would stand empty until it was needed again.

Her last trip to the countryside, to say *au revoir* to Cecile's uncle and aunt and the other families she'd met over the past months. How the children had grown! The noisy farm dogs who'd terrified her at first but now ran up and licked her hands. The smell of Madame Tordi's lavender. The rich, dank smell of the black earth that nurtured the bounty that had sustained the unit. Père Francois's wine.

There had been tears when they'd left, from Rainey, Edna, and Dorothy. But they were happy tears and they brought back good memories. And Dorothy had vowed to come back to Rouen and to the countryside of Normandy again. They'd parked the jeep in the motor pool area and handed over the keys to Johann. He was leaving too, returning to his home on a farm outside Wiesbaden; he and the other POWs would be gone tomorrow before sunrise.

As the women turned to go back to their barracks, Dorothy heard Rainey's voice.

"Dorothy! There's something here for you. A package! It was hidden under the spare."

Dorothy leaned down and looked. Sure enough, in the compartment next to the tire was a square package wrapped in brown paper and tied with string. The name DOROTHY THOM was written in capital letters in black ink. At first she'd thought how lucky it was that Rainey found it—hidden as it was in the wheel well—perhaps that it was a care package from her mother. But no, there wasn't any postage. And this item was sturdy, wooden? She sat down in the courtyard surrounded by the other women and unfolded the paper. The women gasped. It was one of the wooden boxes carved by the POWs. The women called them "gift boxes," even though they looked more like jewelry boxes. Over the past few months, the men had spent their off hours doing crafts to keep their hands and minds occupied. And since many of them were carpenters, little items of beautifully carved wood began to appear in alcoves and back areas around the women's quarters. Exactly how they got there was a mystery, since fraternization between the two sets of occupants of la caserne was strictly verboten. And yet.

Dorothy's box was lovely, exquisitely carved, and intricately made with a mirror inside and gold trim around the edges. It smelled like freshly cut cedar. And there was a small white card inside folded in half. Dorothy opened it and smiled. The printed letters were large and carefully formed in black ink by a strong hand.

To die kleine Frau, with respect and affection.

EPILOGUE

Spring 1996
Musée du Louvre
Paris, France

The museum was crowded, as usual, and there was a traffic jam on the Daru Staircase ("Escalier Daru," Dorothy said) in the Denon Wing leading to the gallery of archaic Greek art. Gum-cracking teens and disorienting rapid-fire camera flashes meshed with annoying Americans, their voices loud and smug, along with the sound of heels on the smooth marble floors that seemed impervious to the cacophony. Of course, they would be unimpressed, worn down as they were by centuries of feet, soldiers, servants, courtiers, and queens. No sound-muffling wall coverings here despite renovation after renovation by men named Louis, Philippe, and Francis. The last—completed in 1600-something—updated a massive sprawling building that began life as a fortress or hunting lodge, depending on which history one read, but never got around to padding the marble and stone to better control sound. The supreme rulers of France's past would have been blasé about the throngs of people and would have recognized the sound of the great hall stairway. They would not have recognized the two women standing on the landing, their faces raised in awe, oblivious to the passing tourists who traded irritated glances their way and muttered, "Excuse me!" in overloud voices.

Dorothy, Leila, and Hazel always met on this stairway. In the fifties, it was like clockwork. Every other year, a trip to Paris except for the year that Leila's son, Paris, had pneumonia and Hazel's eldest had a baby. Thereafter, their meetings were irregular, buffeted by work conflicts and family commitments. Dorothy was a college librarian and professor. Hazel supervised a logistics section at Ft. Knox and Leila was a high school principal. Then, as the years moved on through the eighties, there were the inevitable life signposts to contend with. Doro's husband, Leila's mother, Pearl's heart attack ("They're called 'events' now," Leila commented), Hazel's arthritis. And the world got darker—the visual diminishment that Doro at first thought was just old age transformed into a shadow world that lost the edges of objects, the sparkle in a glance, the uplift of a smile. And Leila's knee—uncooperative at times even when she was younger—decided on its own accord that it had had enough and refused to let her walk at a brisk pace for miles like she used to.

And so, the Paris trip was put off another year for knee replacement and cataract surgery. One heart med was switched out for another. Leila's granddaughter graduated from med school. Hazel downsized to a condo on a golf course. Doro's nephew's business celebrated its tenth year operating in the black. Finally, the dust settled, eleven years had passed, and the travel agent was given her orders. This would be the trip of all trips because it would be the last one. Leila's son was determined to "accompany" her. Doro was advised by well-meaning but clueless nieces and nephews that she couldn't ("He said *shouldn't*! Not the same thing!") travel by herself anymore. Then Hazel had a stroke. Only two now.

After all they'd been through, the lives they'd led, the indignity of being shuttled around like the little old ladies they were was too much to stomach. And the thought of making the journey to this hallowed stairwell and finding out that they were the only one there was an inevitable outcome that these two realists would not accept. Both or none. Now or never. So this would probably be—no, this *would* be the last trip.

They stood in the middle of the stairwell. Ignored the ugly comments and shrugged off the shoves and "Excuse mes!" shouted because it was assumed that they were hard of hearing. Leila, a Jedi Knight with her cane, briefly considered tripping an assailant. Doro, her Coke-bottle-thick-lensed glasses a lifesaver, could still lift weights and wasn't above a reciprocal shove to a younger set of ribs. But the thought of employing jujitsu tactics only lasted a moment. The women's attention was focused solely on one object, a pinnacle of gleaming white marble in the sharp June morning sunlight. The wings spread like miracles above their heads.

They had first seen it in late September 1945, not long after the official Japanese surrender. The second Allied victory. Five months after VE Day, the day that the 6888th Central Postal Directory Battalion marched on parade in the city square of Rouen, France. That day had seemed to be the physical embodiment of their experience for the past three years. Boot camp and marching in the cold rain at Ft. Devens. Root beer floats. Ft. Des Moines. Ft. Huachuca. Combat training at Ft. Oglethorpe. The rock and rolling of the *Île de France* as it maneuvered its way around land mines during a crossing of the North Atlantic. Blackout curtains. A cold, filthy airplane hangar filled to the ceiling with undelivered mail, packages, and rats. An old clock tower in the city center of the old city of Joan of Arc. And le Louvre with its *Winged Victory*—their victory over the Nazis and so much else.

"What do you think, Private First Class Thom?" Leila asked.

Dorothy grinned and shifted her weight from her left foot to her right to ease the ache in her hip. What an adventure this life had been!

"I think it's grand, Branch, I really do."

Now it was Leila's turn to grin, although she felt tears forming in her eyes.

"We did it, didn't we?" she asked, thinking back to the girl that she once was. "We really did it."

"We sure did, Private," Dorothy's voice was strong and firm. "As the girls would say, we had a job to do and we did it."

THE END

Author's Note

No Better Time was inspired by the stories that my cousin Dorothy told of her experiences in the army during World War II along with anecdotes and family lore that made me laugh, frown, and wonder. It was enriched and framed by comments and quotations from a broad landscape of individuals. There is no way that I could include all of their words. Of the many that spent time on my board of inspiration, a few deserve mention.

The 6888th was a postal service unit responsible for processing the mail of military personnel serving in Europe. The women took their mission seriously as is noted in their motto: No mail, low morale. Letters from home were the text messages and email of that time, points of connection that had unmeasurable value. Of this, Dorothy said, "You could see the last time this man received mail. And you were determined to find him."

Pfc. Deloris Ruddock followed up on that sentiment many years later during a ceremony honoring the battalion by saying: "We had a job to do and we did it."

The working title and, in fact, *only* title of my story was inspired by the words of Pressly Holliday, quarter master sergeant, retired, in a letter that he wrote to President Harry S. Truman in September 1945: "I urgently request that you exercise your authority as Commander-in-Chief of the armed forces to direct by executive order the enlistment of Negroes and their organization into units of every branch of the regular army . . . and that this policy be extended to whatever reserves or auxiliary forces may be established as the peace time army . . . If it should be decided to comply with this request no better time than now could be found . . ."

The United States Armed Forces were desegregated by Executive Order 9981 on July 12, 1948. In 1978, the Women's Army Corps and other female units were disbanded, and their members merged into the appropriate branch.

SJW

Acknowledgments

This is a book that might never have been written. It was a jewel of a story, but it was hidden within a treasure vault of many stories. My mother's family, its members scattered across the country, gathered infrequently, but when they did, mercy! When Mom and her cousins became the "elders," family stories were passed along with more urgency. Being the family history geek that I am, I listened and scribbled. "Cousin Dorothy" was my mother's first cousin (her mother and my grandmother were sisters), and she was the keeper of many stories. On her visits to Columbus, Dorothy spent time with Mom and my aunts, Denie and Hattie. Food was prepared, beverages were poured, and laughter was pervasive until our jaws and sides ached. On one particular visit, I reserved time with Dorothy (her popularity demanded it) to get details on the family. In Mom's living room, in a food coma and enjoying myself but armed with pen and paper (no iPad then), I teased Dorothy about her "adventures."

Mom chimed in, "Yes, Dorothy's had some adventures, all right!"

In her elegant yet lighthearted way, Dorothy commented (I'm paraphrasing here): "Oh, I've done a few things in my life." Riotous laughter from my aunts. "I've taught school, third graders; they were sweet. Spelman was fun. I'm studying Spanish now, thinking of writing a book. I went to Paris, drove a truck . . . or was it a Jeep when I was in the army. Then I went to Japan and we . . ."

My pen screeched to a halt.

Wait. What was that she said?

"You were in the army?" I asked.

A nod from Dorothy then, "And we went to the . . ."

I interrupted again. "What's this about you being in the army?"

An insouciant shrug of her shoulders.

"Didn't I mention that before? I was in the army. You knew that."

Um. No.

The notes that I scribbled were one-liners followed by multiple exclamation points. In the years that followed, I wrote other stories, inspired by a variety of scenarios, but I revisited those pages periodically, adding notes in red or highlighting sentences or phrases. I followed up with Dorothy by phone or letter. Her penmanship was exquisite. I kept a photo of Pfc. Dorothy Turner on my desk. *A story I'll write someday*, I thought. *Perhaps.*

The US military never expected to include women in their ranks. Women of color, including African American women, were another resource that the military had not considered. But once the call went out, it was answered. Dorothy served with women from across the country, from Washington State to Florida, from Brooklyn to Los Angeles and all points in between. Sharecroppers daughters, domestic workers, teachers, secretaries, students. They worked together. They looked out for each other. And they became friends for life, forming the National Association of Black Military Women. Dorothy looked forward to their conferences and attended with enthusiasm even when she was in her eighties. Sisters for life.

It is this sisterhood that spoke loudest to me when I chose to write this book. I researched military protocol (thank you Bruce Smith, Ron Ellis, and others); I excavated the notes on my mother's side of the family; I time-traveled through the 1940s and felt the rough fabric of khakis and the unyielding leather of the ubiquitous boots. I consulted books and videos, and listened to the interviews given by veterans. I dug up my notes from conversations with my father who served with the 332nd, a.k.a. the Tuskegee Airmen, at Ramitelli in Italy (Dad was a mechanic) and my father-in-law who served in the Pacific Theatre (Hawaii, Okinawa) with the regiment that owed its existence to the Harlem Hellfighters of World War I, the 369th. I dug up notes from the Civil War experiences of Dad's family as well, men who served with the US Colored Troops (USCT) and the Massachusetts 55th. There is a common thread running through *all* of these narratives, and that is the personal one. Each veteran utters a version of the following: "I was friends with this girl (or guy) who . . ." Friendship, sisterhood, collaboration—the word "we" was my searchlight. I was taken with the ways that the WACs looked after each other, the older women (older being early thirties) kept an eye on the younger ones, and the sharing of secrets and advice.

I hope that the reader will accept the leaps of imagination I've taken: Dorothy's commentary was full of one-liners and there were many times when I had to read between the lines. This is a work of fiction. I have been inspired by and borrowed from family lore—and modified it to suit my purposes!—as well as soldiers' memories recounted by Dorothy and many others. Dorothy's adventurous spirit was contagious: if Dorothy did it, then her younger cousins, my mother and aunts, were inspired to do it too! And that was passed on to the next generation as well. Take risks. Use your passport! Go to school. Meet people and enjoy the richness of life.

My thanks go to Dorothy Turner Johnson (1915–2015) for taking a moment to clarify that nugget of gold buried within the narrative of her life. I am grateful to the Veterans History Project and the Library of Congress, which houses video and audio interviews of women who served in World War II, including some who served with the 6888th Central Postal Directory Battalion. In one of the interviews, Dorothy appears, wearing a fabulous hat! Thank you to those who helped me along the journey of writing this book: Nita Walker, MD, for advice and guidance with medical protocol and background; Ron Ellis, writer, colleague, and army veteran, who graciously agreed on short notice to spot-check chapters for me when I was against a deadline. To Ron goes the credit for the line, "If it's moving, salute it!" To my family, I send my gratitude. They are always a source of delight, and especially to my favorite sister, Claire Williams, more gratitude than I can express. She is my only sister, but that's beside the point.

Thank you to my agent, Matt Bialer, for patience and insight. To my editor, Patrik Henry Bass, I do not know what I would do without you. You have been a guiding light through my storytelling journeys. The amazing professionals at Amistad/HarperCollins make this all look so easy: Francesca Walker, assistant editor, what would I do without your patience and super assistance with the tech goblins; Brieana Garcia, associate director of marketing, who knows more about what I should be doing on social media than anyone; the amazing Ashley Yepsen, associate director of publicity—I am more grateful than I can say; and Stephen Brayda, art director, thank you for bringing out the heart of my story with your thoughtful cover design.

When I first considered writing a story inspired by Dorothy's experience, my husband, Bruce Smith, once a first lieutenant in the army, thought it was a fine idea. He recounted his own experiences (unlike Dorothy, he did *not* think that combat training was "exciting") and clarified the mysteries of some of the acronyms used. Throughout our marriage, Bruce was present in the truest sense of the word. He was the jet engine beneath my wings, encouraging me and making sure that I took care of myself during what often is a long writing process. Bruce died in June 2022. For this, I don't have the words. But I will be grateful to him all of my life.

SJW

About the Author

Sheila Williams is the author of seven novels, including *Things Past Telling*, *The Secret Women*, and *Dancing on the Edge of the Roof*, which was adapted for the Netflix film *Juanita*. In addition to her published works, she is the librettist for *Fierce*, an opera commissioned by the Cincinnati Opera. Sheila lives in northern Kentucky.